David Helwig

David Helwig was born in Toronto in 1938. He has lived in Hamilton, Niagara-on-the-Lake, Toronto, Kingston, and in London and Liverpool in England. For some time he taught English at Queen's University and from 1967-69 was involved in teaching at Collins Bay Penitentiary. Between 1974 and 1976, he was Literary Manager of CBC Television Drama. His first publication was a story in *Canadian Forum* when he was an undergraduate, and he has been writing steadily since. His novels include *Jennifer, A Sound Like Laughter, It Is Always Summer,* and *The King's Evil.* He has also published six books of poetry, among them *Atlantic Crossings* and *A Book of the Hours.*

Barbara Astman

Barbara Astman was born in 1950 in Rochester, New York and has resided in Toronto since 1970. After studying at the Rochester Institute of Technology, she continued her education in Toronto at the Ontario College of Art, where she is presently on faculty. Her work, which has been exhibited nationally and internationally, ranges from autobiographical narrative art to personalized architectural forms.

New Press Canadian Classics

Distinguished by the use of Canadian fine art on its covers, New Press Canadian Classics is an innovative, much-needed series of high-quality, reasonably priced editions of the very best Canadian fiction, nonfiction and poetry.

New Press Canadian Classics

Hubert Aquin *The Antiphonary*
  Alan Brown (trans.)

Marie-Claire Blais *Nights in the Underground*
  Ray Ellenwood (trans.)

George Bowering *Burning Water*

Matt Cohen *The Expatriate*

Jack David & Robert Lecker (eds.) *Canadian Poetry*
  Volumes One and Two

Mavis Gallant *My Heart Is Broken*

Anne Hébert *Kamouraska*
  Norman Shapiro (trans.)

David Helwig *The Glass Knight, Jennifer*

Robert Kroetsch *Badlands, The Studhorse Man*

Félix Leclerc *The Madman, the Kite & the Island*
  Philip Stratford (trans.)

Keith Maillard *Alex Driving South, Two Strand River*

Antonine Maillet *Pélagie*
  Philip Stratford (trans.)

Brian Moore *An Answer From Limbo*

Michael Ondaatje *Coming Through Slaughter*

Leon Rooke *Fat Woman*

George Ryga *The Ecstasy of Rita Joe and other plays*

new press CANADIAN CLASSICS

David Helwig

The Glass Knight

General Publishing Co. Limited
Toronto, Canada

Copyright © 1976 by David Helwig

For Anne and Michael

Oberon Press edition
published in 1976

General Paperbacks edition
published in 1983

ISBN 0-7736-7046-7

Printed and bound in Canada

One

Elizabeth, wherever you are,

I am waiting. No, past waiting. I am almost past caring that I do not know where you are. It is daylight on a December morning. I am here, writing this to you. And somehow you are here or I could not write to you, talk to you. Have I discovered something or am I only in that state of tiredness when obvious things take on too much meaning, factitious resonance?

It would not be better if things happened to men just as they wish. Is that profound or banal? I am past knowing. Maybe it is both.

On the wall is that snapshot of the two of us in Ottawa. I am past anger too.

Where are you? Suddenly I am afraid again. I think of all the years of my life when you did not exist. Sometimes you were impossible and yet you came to be. Is there something to be learned from this? From anything?

Time is a child moving counters in a game. The royal power is a child's.

Where are you? In me, in my mind, in my mind's eye, yes, but where are you? I must sleep now. My eyes are closing. I will pursue you into dreams and find you there. Or not.

2

Elizabeth's photograph album:

The summer before she left home, the garden of her parents' house. Tom and her mother sit in folding chairs, Tom's mobile face shaping itself around an idiotic grin. Her mother wears a pale pink dress with a pattern of checks. Her mother smiles as if she has been told to smile. Tom is wearing a blue sweatshirt, his bare arms tanned, apparently hairless, for the camera could not see the fine blond hairs. Behind the two chairs a bush of red floribunda roses. The back of the garden shaded, blue. The plastic of the empty chair to which Elizabeth will return is blue and white,

her roommate in her first year at university. Fall, the leaves in Macdonald Park bright, mostly yellow, in an afternoon sunlight that is slanted and rich. Pamela stands between two trees and smiles at the camera. She is wearing jeans and a purple blouse. She has short legs and a heavy body, a plain round face, beautiful thick dark brown hair. In the distance is a small patch where the lake shows through,

Elizabeth herself. It is summer again. She is sitting on the dock at the cottage. Behind her the brown wall of the cottage, the white-frame screen door. Elizabeth is wearing a new white bikini, and she is smiling at the camera. Her hair is in a braid. In the far corner of the picture is Philip's dog. He is white, and his name is Grump. Philip, who is twelve, took the picture, and it is crooked,

her father, climbing out of the car at the front of the house. It is a sunny day, but her father seems to have something else on his mind, although he has turned toward the camera and smiled. His right hand is on the car door, and he is wearing a dark suit. His face is handsome, solid, and he looks young. Two days after the picture is taken he is dead, and Elizabeth only sees the picture when she gets the film developed months later,

Pam and her boyfriend, John Langdon, stand with their arms around each other outside of John's flat on Barrie Street. Burtch, his roommate, is waving out the window,

John and Pam and Burtch and Walter and Janey on a beach on the St. Lawrence. They are all eating, and Burtch, who blinked at the wrong moment, has his eyes closed. Pam's arm is blurred as it moves to point at something across the blue water. The summer sun is very bright on the sand,

Tom, in Ottawa at Christmastime last year. He looks older

and is wearing an overcoat,

Elizabeth, last summer, riding her bicycle in front of the courthouse. She is wearing denim shorts and a white blouse. There is an old man standing in front of the limestone courthouse watching her or watching Burtch, who is taking the picture. Elizabeth is smiling in an odd way because she is concentrating on riding the bicycle. The slope of green grass behind her is pale, a little dead and bleached because it is August,

a street in Kingston. The street is empty, and the picture is not very interesting except for the upper corner, where the summer sunlight is shining toward the camera through a tree, and the leaves and sun form a golden blur. In the foreground there are cars parked, and two empty metal garbage cans,

Robert, sitting on the rocks at Lake Ontario Park. In the distance is a line of horizon that is Wolfe Island. The water is darker blue than the sky, and the island is no colour at all, merely a darkening in the blue space. Robert is looking out across the water, looking away from the camera. He is wearing a green sweater, and his arms are around his knees. This is the first picture Elizabeth ever took of him, and she could only take it secretly, from behind.

Two

Robert had almost decided to stay away. Already the day had been one of those when he could make sense of nothing. Marion had phoned again, demanding that he come to Toronto to visit their father, who lay in the family house senile and dying. Robert said Yes, sometime, hung up the phone, tried to read Freud again, just reading occasional sentences and paragraphs from *Civilization and its Discontents*. Thought of Freud refusing pain-killers because he thought they muddled his thinking.

As the summer night outside his window began to darken, he went out and began to walk through the gradually cooling air of the streets near his apartment.

In the west there was a strange band of yellow across the sky where the sun had set, and ahead of Robert a boy and girl walked along the street holding hands. The girl was a head taller than the boy, almost as tall and thin as Robert himself.

The boy and girl looked toward him and spoke to each other. He turned a corner to a street where he was alone under the trees. How had he come to this? What had happened? Even now he wasn't sure.

He and Jennifer had come to Kingston after a year when it was hard for them to be in the same room. Kingston was supposed to be a new start, but they both knew within a month that they had brought the past in their suitcases, and all the wounds had reopened.

Then another beginning with Molly.

Robert stood at the corner of the street where the party was being held. He hated going to parties alone. He disliked watching some of the more grotesque sexual conjunctions preparing themselves.

Robert walked down the street, past the door of the apartment building and down as far as the next corner; he didn't want to be alone, but he didn't want to tell any lies, he didn't want to be charming or pleasant. For a moment he was tempted to phone Jennifer, and the anger at himself that this produced sent him back to the door of the apartment building and up the three flights of stairs to the party.

It was always the same party, darkness, music lost in the sound of voices, bodies crowded together. In a corner by an open window a couple of people were smoking dope.

As he made his way toward the kitchen to find a drink, Robert saw Kitty Nelson and her man, a balding graduate student that everybody called Toad, waving to him across a crowd.

"I heard from Molly," Kitty said as she came across and took Robert by the arm. "She and Andrew just had a baby."

Robert looked down at her. The nipples of her small breasts showed through the green material of her blouse. On her eyelids there was a quantity of dark makeup that made her face look dirty. As Robert's eyes moved away from her, unable to watch her face as she spoke to him, he noticed a girl in a corner of the room, her skin looking bright and clean beside her black hair, her green eyes watching him, a rather tall, elegant girl that he'd seen the year before when he delivered a guest lecture on book editing to a class in bibliography. She had been the most striking girl in the class, and in the few months since, he had watched her riding her bicycle through the streets around the university, his fascination with her growing. He thought of her as the Bicycle Girl. Now and then he asked other people if they'd noticed her, but no-one but himself seemed to have.

As their eyes met, the girl smiled. Kitty noticed that Robert wasn't paying attention to what she was saying and followed the glance of his eyes backward to where the girl stood.

"Molly said she might get down for a visit sometime in the fall. I'd love to see the baby. I really want to have children. I can't wait. I know girls aren't supposed to want to any more, but I do. I want to have two cute little baby boys. Isn't that vulgar and ordinary?"

Robert and Molly had agreed not to write, and he was torn now between the desire for her to mention Molly again, poking the sore and making it hurt, and the more sane desire for her to be quiet and let him go away. Looking at Kitty, seeing her nipples under the cloth, made him imagine a child at Molly's breast, and he was jealous of the child and at the same time obscurely wished that it were his.

Kitty went on talking to him, but he couldn't bring himself to pretend to listen to her. He looked down, still avoiding her eyes, and found himself staring at her bare feet, the little fat toes, the curious roundness of the arch. He looked up again; the girl was gone. He wanted to find her and talk to her. It was too much to hope that she was at the party by herself, but it would be pleasant to talk to her; he'd been alone too long.

He told Kitty that he needed a drink and made his way to the kitchen. There would be no gin, of course. He should have brought some. The refrigerator was full of beer, and he took a bottle though he didn't much like beer. With the open bottle in his hand, he began to look for the Bicycle Girl, but there was no sign of her in the kitchen or in the small bedroom that opened off the kitchen. He avoided conversations with a couple of people he knew and walked through the apartment until he saw her standing in a hallway, talking to a short girl with blond hair. She looked toward him as she talked, and he knew that she wanted him to talk to her, and he was pleased. As the girl with blond hair moved away, Robert walked across to her.

"You're the most beautiful girl at the party, so I was determined to talk to you."

"I wanted to talk to you too. Sometimes I know as soon as I see people that I want to meet them." Where they were standing in the hall, there was no crowd and it seemed almost quiet.

Her eyes were big and set wide apart and were an odd colour between green and grey. She had a strange mouth, and Robert's first thought as he noticed it was that as she grew older her mouth would grow ugly. For some reason that fascinated him.

"Are you here with someone or could we go for a walk?"

"I'd like to go outside. It's hot in here. I don't like parties much."

"Let's go down by the lake," he said.

She nodded.

As they walked down the stairs, he felt that he didn't have to speak, to make any kind of gesture. When they got outside, he noticed a wind in the treetops, and she pointed out stars to him, first Polaris and the constellation of Cassiopeia, then going on to others less familiar.

"Where did you learn them?" he said.

"My father"

"Is he an astronomer?"

"No, he was just an amateur observer. He died a couple of years ago."

From above they could hear the muted voices of the party.

They turned toward the lake and walked the few blocks to the park in front of City Hall and sat on the rocks looking across the marina toward Wolfe Island where a few white lights and the high red lights of the broadcasting tower showed in the dark. Out in the water the lights of the ferry moved slowly toward them.

"I've been watching you all this summer," he said. "I think of you as the Bicycle Girl."

"It's not even my bike. I borrowed it from a friend for the summer. I call it Jupiter."

"Why?"

"It has a certain dignity."

They sat in silence as the ferry came closer, gradually changing from a set of moving lights to a squat boat on which they could see the shapes of cars and passengers.

"Do you ever find," the girl said, "that everything goes

13

away from you sometimes? That you're just not there any more or the world's got nothing for you, that it's just blank and grey and vague?"

"Sometimes a little."

"That happens to me. I hate it. Sometimes when it happens I get desperate. I feel that I'd do anything to make myself feel something. I do silly things and hurt people. But I have to do something."

"It's better to do something."

She stared out across the lake. The slanted light from a lamp-post on the ferry dock emphasized her prominent cheek-bones.

"Sometimes I'm fascinated with the water," she said. "I mean the idea of drowning. Some of my friends say that I'm just being morbid, but it isn't that. A friend of mine who's studied psychology always starts talking about the unconscious mind. I haven't read enough. I never quite catch up."

Her eyes draw my heart, her words like a song where the meaning is not in the words at all. I am happy and I am afraid.

"I frighten my mother when I talk about drowning because she thinks I mean suicide and I'm unhappy. It isn't just that. Often I'm not even sad, or I don't feel sad or depressed, but it's like something pulling me, as if some voice was saying it's time to die. Do you understand what I mean? I always wonder if people understand me. Two summers ago I was in England, and one night, going to a play, there was a Greek Orthodox priest, at least I guess he was, he had a beard and robes, but he was young, almost as young as me, and all of a sudden I wanted to talk to him and tell him what I'm telling you, but I didn't. I just got off the tube and went to the play. Sometimes when I talk to my friends, they just shake their heads at me. Do you understand?"

She turned and looked at him.

"Yes," Robert said.

"Yes to what?" she said.

"Anything. You."

"Do you really understand what I mean?"

"I understand that you mean it."

He reached out and touched her face. She turned away.

"What's the matter?"

"I'm frigid," she said.

Just like that.

"I don't think you are."

"Why not?"

"No-one is, not really."

"My father said something like that once."

He touched her cheek and took his hand away.

"I had an abortion when I was nineteen, and I've been frigid ever since. Maybe I was before. I don't remember. My father said it would go away when I was ready."

Robert could feel it now, how her trust drew him in, built a wall around the two of them, imprisoned him and set him free.

When a woman tells me the truth about herself, she dances naked before me, and I am defenceless.

"Did your father die suddenly?"

"He had a heart attack. Ever since then my mother seems to be frightened of everything. But especially for me and my brother. I guess she's afraid of being left alone. She's spent her whole life looking after people. She was a nurse before she got married, and she made her family the centre of everything. Now she's afraid that she'll be left alone."

"But if she was ever left alone, she'd probably be fine."

"She doesn't think so."

"There are always bedpans to empty, for those who want to empty them."

She was silent, turned away. He was furious, wanted to flay her for her mother's commonplace self-sacrifice. Young girls and their families, the only things they knew, the only language they had for destiny.

15

"I've made you angry," he said.

"I thought you understood."

"I'm a bad-tempered man."

"Why?"

"It must be chemical." He heard himself laughing, wondered why.

"After the abortion our doctor wanted to give me tranquilizers, but I wouldn't take them."

"Why?"

"I don't really know. My mother takes sleeping-pills. It makes me angry. Sometimes I fight with her about it, but it does no earthly good. There are so many things I don't say to her because she'll be frightened or upset."

Robert looked out across the dark water, where once again the ferry was a pattern of distant lights.

"The water's so beautiful in the dark," she said, "so soft. When I'm swimming I love to dive down under the water until I think my lungs are going to break me open. Do you like that?"

"I don't swim very well. I never learned to swim underwater. When I was young my mother was afraid of beaches and didn't want me to learn to swim. When I was older I was embarrassed so I avoided swimming unless I was alone."

"I used to race when I was at camp. I won a lot of races. The competition wasn't very stiff there."

"Whose child was it, when you had the abortion?"

"The boy next door. Not really next door, he lived around the corner."

"Did you ever want to keep it?"

"I don't think so. I don't know if I ever thought about it. My father was an assistant deputy minister who knew everybody. He arranged it. When I think about it now, I can't really believe it happened the way it did. I always think that I made it up or saw it in a movie."

"That happens with the past, doesn't it? We lose it all."

16

"I keep a diary and all sorts of old photographs so that I won't lose things."

"But it still turns into pictures. Like your abortion. There's no way for you to get your hands on it. It's just gone."

"I could tell you all the details, but you're right, they're like something that happened to someone else."

"Tomorrow maybe you'll remember this conversation, and it will be like that."

"No."

"Why not?"

"It just won't."

Tiny waves slapped softly on the rock at their feet. The lights of the ferry went on through the darkness.

"Why don't you walk home with me, and I'll make some tea?"

Robert nodded, and they stood up. Turned from the dark water and back to the city. A couple of blocks away, there was a sound of shouting and singing. The beverage rooms were closing at the Frontenac and the Prince George, and the noise of the drinkers echoed in the empty streets. Robert and the girl walked side by side, not speaking. At a stop-light a car pulled up beside them to wait for the green light, and heads turned, theirs, the others. Strangers, a man and woman together.

They walked through streets of old brick and stone houses, Tory Kingston still flourishing in some of the houses, others rundown, rooms and apartments. She lived in one of these, only a block and a half from the apartment where Molly and Andrew had lived.

As they walked up the dark stairs toward her room, Robert remembered what she had said about being frigid and wondered if it was true or only something she said to avoid awkwardness. Robert had been alone too long, and the dark stairway seemed full of sexual suggestion, possible touchings, encounters.

On the second landing, she turned on a light and took a ring of keys out of her pocket. Her odd mouth was drawn down in a frown of concentration for a moment as she sorted the keys, then she turned to Robert, her face opening, as she turned the key in the lock and opened the door.

The room dark, then light, blue and white, pale, neat, still. Robert walked in and felt himself an intruder, out of rhythm with the place, too tall, too nervous. She shook back her long hair and in that gesture took possession.

"Do you want tea?"

He nodded and looked for someplace to sit. A wicker rocker or the bed. It was a room for one person, a chosen solitude. The books and papers on the desk were neatly laid out. As he crossed the room, he caught a glimpse of himself passing through the mirror over the dressing-table, like a ghost. He sat on the bed. The girl's tall body moved through the room, neatly, familiar with all the shapes, fitting her movement to them easily.

She poured water into an electric kettle, and as she waited for it to boil took out a brown teapot and a package of tea-bags. Two cups that matched the pot. As she made the tea, her gestures were economical, easy.

There was a curious emptiness as they sat down with their cups. Robert was unused to drinking tea, and the strange taste, green, metallic, set his mouth on edge. The room seemed larger, emptier than the dark space beside the water, and their few sentences could not fill it. Robert found himself looking at her hands, which were large with broad fingernails, trimmed short. She held both of them around the teacup. Robert realized that he didn't know her name. He didn't want to ask. He didn't want to know her.

She looked up from her tea.

"We don't really know each other, do we?" she said.

"That's what I was thinking," he said.

"Sometimes I think the only way I'd ever stop being frigid

is with a stranger."

"Why?"

"I guess I think I wouldn't be myself."

Robert put down his cup and went to the chair where she was sitting. He put his hands on the back of her head, but she shook her head and pulled away from him.

"Am I not stranger enough?"

"It's just an idea. Don't be angry."

"I'm not. Maybe puzzled."

"Me too."

He went and sat on the bed. They drank their tea in silence. The warmth of the tea in his stomach and something else, something happening in his head, made Robert suddenly sleepy. The room was disappearing.

"I think I should go," he said.

She nodded.

"I'm glad I met you," she said. The look in her eyes hurt him. Robert stood up, said goodnight, walked to the door. As he opened it and walked out, he didn't look back. Down dark stairs, out another door to the street, hurrying away. But when he reached the street, he stopped and looked up at the lighted window.

2

It would not be incorrect to suggest that the Wordsworthan sublime like the demonic sublime in Dickens is in which it was to be, by and large, expected to be achieved by the trans-position of material from the genre the ethos of another genetic mode.

Robert stared at the page. The linotype operator must have been drunk. It was the worst set of proofs he'd ever read. Besides that, the book was written in double talk. He'd said so when the manuscript first came in, but the academic experts called the book important, and Robert had tried to get the style improved in a series of letters that grew more and more turgid until Robert gave up.

It wasn't his responsibility. He reminded himself of the reasons he had come here, to this unimportant editorial job, to escape large decisions, worrying responsibilities. In Toronto where his decisions cost money, his nerves had begun to go to pieces. Sometimes his vision would blur, he couldn't sleep, his head ached. So he had chosen to retreat to a mechanical job that cost him nothing but occasional irritation; a deliberate step down, away from challenges.

He saw Ray Statler's figure move past the door, in a flash of bright colours. He was the new graphic designer, just out of art school, the first designer hired by the university press after years of contracting out their books. Statler's trousers all seemed to be either pink or purple and he tended to wear them with yellow or green shirts and ties of dark red or black. Just to look at his outfits was exhausting. He was an ambitious young man, with some talent and excessive self-confidence. He had told Robert in almost their first conversation that his former girlfriend had gone to Europe and he was on the look-out for a replacement. To be his mistress, clearly, was to be regarded as a splendid opportunity, and within a few weeks he had found a beautiful Czech girl with long dark hair and soulful eyes. A kind of Slovak princess. Ray accepted her astonishing beauty as no more than his due. They did make a handsome couple, for Ray had good features and reddish golden hair and beard, but Robert found it hard to believe that either one of them really existed.

They belonged on the pages of a magazine. They didn't exist firmly enough to make him jealous that they were young and beautiful and that he was tall and skinny and big featured with thinning hair and weakening muscles.

Outside the window of the little house where the press had

its offices, the grass and trees were still vibrant green in the September sunlight. Here and there a few leaves were turning yellow but it was still really summer. In a neighbour's yard, the bright flares of the zinnias hung in the light. Robert turned his head and Ray Statler appeared in the doorway.

"How are things?" he said.

"This is the worst set of proofs I've ever seen. The linotype operator must have been drunk."

"Those people are a pain in the ass. We gotta move to someplace else. Christ, they can't do much, and what they do, they do badly. There's a new outfit called Computex that I want to try. Get the type set there and print at that outfit in Barrie. It's stupid to work in letterpress these days unless you want to do limited editions."

"Have you convinced Wilson?"

"I've discussed it with him four times and I still don't know what he thinks."

"You never will."

"I'm going to do it whether he likes it or not."

"Oh he'll let you do it. Or at least he won't stop you. But if something goes wrong he'll be able to claim it was all your idea and that he never gave it approval."

"So he'll let me do whatever I like?"

"Pretty much."

"Good. That's all I care about."

"I have a kind of picture of Wilson walking through the world backward bent over to cover his tracks."

"Perfect way to get buggered by the future."

Ray sat down in one of the office chairs.

"Can I sit down?" he said. After the fact.

"I'd rather do anything than work."

Statler leaned back, gave a self-satisfied stretch and yawn, arms and legs spread as if offering himself to any goddess who might be passing, hot with desire for just such a lovely golden body.

"Ever read any Czech poetry?" he said.

Robert shook his head. It was inevitable that the conversation should be about something he was ignorant of.

"Margita's been translating some for me to read. It's good. It's funny how you can feel right away that it's European. There's a poem about Edison, by Nezval. Only a European could have written it. For them America's still waiting to be discovered. I told Margita she should do a whole book of translations and we could put them out through the press. I could do woodcuts to illustrate them."

"Are they good translations?"

"Yeah. She's really bright. I've only had to make a few suggestions here and there."

Passing goddess, tear out his tongue. To hear him patronize his lovely dark princess will kill me. I hunch misshapen in my chair and watch the autumn sunlight catch the edge of his golden hair. I see them both at the edge of some fairy tale.

"Do you want a cup of coffee, Robert? I'll make some if you like."

"Sure," Robert said, knowing that it was a mistake to drink coffee, but somehow unable to say no. Statler was making him irritable but he didn't want him to go away. Didn't know why.

Statler got up and went to the little kitchen of the house where they kept an electric kettle, instant coffee and occasionally cookies or a piece of cheese. At 10.30 every morning Wilson's secreatry made coffee for them all, but at other times during the day they made their own. Robert stared out the window where the afternoon sunlight came across the trees and into the office, pouring itself on the chair where Ray Statler had been sitting. And on one half of Cindy's picture that hung on the wall, illuminating the left side of the round smiling face, a corner of a red dress with a white collar that set off the delicate colouring of the child's skin. Beside, in the shade, was Gavin, his son, his face smiling with a kind of eager boyish handsomeness that might turn into anything. He was small for his age, oddly, and worried about it. Robert tried to re-assure him that he would be sure to inherit some of his father's height, but the boy knew that his maternal grandfather had been small.

Robert had left the Toronto job and come to Kingston hoping the improvement in his nerves would make him a better father to his children, but before that could happen, he had moved out. He wondered how the children felt about Jennifer's lovers. He didn't want to know these things.

Robert turned to his desk and had corrected a few more lines of the proofs when Ray Statler came in with two mugs of coffee, put one down on the desk and sat back down in the sunlight with the other. The sun now shone on his face, and he put his head back and spoke with his eyes closed.

"Are you planning to settle down here?" he said.

"I haven't thought that far ahead. My kids are still here. I'm comfortable enough for now."

"You told me you left a better job for this one."

"I don't like pressure."

"I love it. There isn't enough here. I need the experience, but within a year or so, I'm going to screw off and get something better."

Robert nodded.

"Books aren't really my field anyway. Designing books is for old men. You have more fun in a faster game."

"I don't," Robert said. "You might." He lifted the mug to his lips. The coffee was strong and tasted good in his mouth, but he knew what it would do to his stomach. Swallowed.

"Aren't you lonely," Statler said. Robert was shocked by the brashness of the question, yet in a way he was pleased. It seemed to be the question he had wanted someone to ask him for a long time.

"Sometimes," he said. "But I'm getting used to it. I want a bit of rest before I explore any more emotional jungles." Robert was on the point of saying more, but the words were less than half true, and he silenced himself.

"Margita and I were talking about you last night. Actually she was asking me about you. You puzzle her."

"I'm pretty ordinary," Robert said.

'Nobody's ordinary," Statler said complacently.

Robert drank his coffee.

"I told her," Statler said, "that I thought you were one of those people whose talent and intelligence had never really found a shape to express themselves."

Again Robert was startled by the man's presumption, but teased by it, for it might contain the truth.

"How long has Margita been in Canada?"

"Six years. She went to high school here. Her English is almost perfect, isn't it?"

Robert lifted his cup, his eyes moving to the back yard, where a cat was climbing along the edge of the old garage. He thought of the girl again, the Bicycle Girl. She had often come back to his mind in the last two weeks but he hadn't tried to see her, had thought of it but refused himself. In the drawer of the desk in front of him was a picture of Molly. Somewhere in the closet of his apartment was a picture of Jennifer. He didn't want any other pictures yet. For now he wanted to hug his loneliness.

"I've been doing some cover sketches for that book," Statler said, indicating the proofs that lay on the desk. "I figure we need something bright on the cover to make it look better than it is. Something abstract. I think the whole book's a crock of shit, to tell the truth. God, this place gets me down sometimes. You're the only person here worth talking to, and you're not exactly cheerful. We should go out and get drunk together. We'll pick you up a pretty young thing in a bar somewhere and get your ashes hauled." He took a drink of his coffee, emptying the cup. "Time to go and do something marvellous," he said as he stood up. He walked out the door, and into the kitchen where he washed his cup. Robert could hear him whistling between his teeth as he dried it and put it away.

Robert turned to the proofs. His stomach was beginning to hurt from the strong coffee. As he went over the proofs, line by line, correcting the multitude of mistakes, he wondered if Ray was right about his needing a girl. It was nearly a year now since Molly had left. Sometimes, as he wandered around his apartment putting things in order, it seemed to him that he had become an old maid, fussy and fantastical, combining small habits with shapeless imaginings, haunted by succubi, his satisfactions mechanical and poor.

Page after page he put the proofs in order. He would have to see a second set of galleys, and it would add a few weeks' delay to the book's schedule. The author would complain, but Wilson could handle that. It was his *métier*; delay, confusion, evasion, obfuscation, these composed the element in which he swam.

The galleys moved toward their end. Robert reached the final chapter, ten pages that he had never understood. They seemed to him to have little to do with the rest of the book and to be so abstract, written with so little reference to concrete evidence, that the reader knew the author meant something, but had no idea what it could be.

Robert suspected that he was getting hungry, but the pain in his stomach from the coffee was bad enough that he couldn't really tell. He looked at his watch. It was after 4.30. They didn't always keep very regular office hours, but this book was already later than it was supposed to be. Still, if he began with it first thing in the morning, he could have it sent out sometime tomorrow. It certainly wasn't worth a lot of effort to get it to the printer one day earlier. He tossed aside his pencil and turned to the window. The angled sunlight was defining a space of edges and deep dimensions.

This leaf on this tree on this grass by this fence. Everything is precise, has its place in the light. I have limitations, but no shape.

Robert stood up from the desk and went to the cupboard where he'd hung the old baggy cardigan he'd worn to work that morning. On his way out, he had to pass Wilson Beattie's office, and as he passed he heard Wilson's hoarse whisper say his name. He stopped and went toward the open door.

"Rushing off somewhere, Robert?"

"No. Just for a walk and then home."

He entered Wilson's room. It was a handsome office, with low bookshelves filled mostly with books of their own press. On the wall behind Wilson's desk was a George Stubbs painting of a horse, a handsome black stallion, looking sleek against a dark green background, his tail cropped. On the other walls were eighteenth-century prints, a Rowlandson, a couple of late issues of Hogarth, a Bartolozzi, one of the prints adapted from Holbein. The desk was large, antique mahogany with gold-embossed leather on the top; it was Wilson's own desk, which he had brought in to replace the functional piece issued to him a few years before when the press had expanded and moved into this old house. For years before that it had been a one-man operation and Wilson had worked from a small office on the top floor of the Arts Building. He had come to the University from the Library of Parliament where he had taken work after an abortive academic career in history. On the desk sat a rack of pipes, a humidor and a small brass container for pens and pencils. The rich colour of it all, the red, brown and gold, made Wilson look even smaller and paler than he was. His face was an odd whitish colour that made his red lips noticeable, almost as if he were wearing makeup.

"I expect that Traviss book tries your patience," he said. His small face moved through a shifting of lips and eyebrows that brought it close to a smile.

"Don't tease me, Wilson. You know how bad it is."

"Well, you and I don't pretend to be experts in that field, Robert. We had opinions from several very eminent people. No doubt Traviss' style leaves something to be desired, but you did a lot of excellent work on that."

The hint of a smile had disappeared; Wilson was always serious about press business, though Robert wondered from time to time what might be going on in his mind.

Wilson took a pipe from his desk rack and began the lengthy ritual of lighting it. It was while watching Wilson that Robert had decided that all pipe smokers were obsessive-compulsive neurotics; there was a note in his card file about it, but he'd never found a use for the observation. Likely someone else had already made it. He knew that there was no point in expecting Wilson to speak till he was done, so he relaxed in his chair and waited. The pain in his stomach was going away now.

On the third match and after a couple of experimental sucks, Wilson seemed satisfied that the pipe was going.

"Edith would like you to come to dinner this Saturday. Are you still free?"

"I'm always free these days." Robert laughed, nervously, absurdly.

Wilson nodded. He accepted self-pity with as much tolerance as he accepted everything else. His decorum seemed to fit his as easily as the clothes made by his old tailor somewhere in Toronto. He made Robert feel in every way ungainly. Wilson and Ray Statler each wore the style of his generation with ease and comfort; Robert wandered in some middle world.

"We'll say 7 for 7.30, shall we?"

"That's fine, Wilson."

Wilson began to work on the pipe again, set fire to it once or twice more, puffed out a thin stream of smoke. Robert waited patiently.

"Young Statler wants to make some changes."

"He told me this afternoon. I was complaining about the linotype operator who did those Traviss proofs. They're appalling."

"I suppose I must speak to Bert Whitehead. He's been sending us slovenly work lately. I believe things have been going rather badly for him all round. Suppose I'm old-fashioned in my attachment to letterpress, but I must say I associate these new techniques with shoddy work. When photo-offset first began we thought of it as not much better than a mimeograph machine. All the crafts are passing away."

Robert looked across the desk at Wilson's hands, clean, bony, surprisingly large.

"But I suppose the board's decision to hire Statler was in some part an attempt to sharpen us up. Though we're not a business. Whatever it is we are. Neither fish nor fowl, it often seems to me. A fabulous beast, part one thing, part another."

He put down the pipe.

"Don't let me keep you, Robert, if you want to go. Once I begin to talk it's hard to stop myself."

"I think I'll take a walk down by the lake."

"Good idea. It's a fine day. I'll tell Edith to expect you on Saturday night."

Robert walked out the door of the small brick house and turned toward the lake, wondering as he walked through the now-just-cooling air, what, if anything, Wilson had wanted from him. Was he trying to create some kind of conflict, to get Robert on his side against young Statler? Wilson moved by indirection, and as soon as an intention seemed to become clear, he shifted the thrust. Perhaps his intention was always to avoid being tied down in any way.

The traffic on King Street was heavy, and Robert did not look at the water as he waited to cross. He wanted to save it. Finally a break in traffic allowed him to cross the road and the narrow corridor of grass to the sidewalk at the edge of the lake where he stood leaning against the iron fence. The lake was brilliant blue in the early evening sunlight. He looked across at the island. The trees and houses were small and clear, every detail sharply focused.

As if I could walk across the water and reach the island and say Yes, this is the place I wished to be.

Out on the lake he saw a single sailboat, the arch of its white sail drawing it down the course of the wind. Jennifer had never chosen to hear him, to let his mind truly touch her. Always she turned aside and chose silence and left him raging. So he had been turned back into himself, into a confused landscape of muddled insights, now and then dragging one to light, bringing it like a hunter his kill and faced again with silence. The few misshapen essays lay somewhere in a drawer.

He climbed through the iron bars and onto a pile of rocks at the water's edge. He began to toss stones into the water, aiming each to land at the exact centre of the spreading circle of ripples left by the previous stone. When the handful of stones was gone, he stared across the water at the white sail that was moving away toward the island, and as he stood up, turning to leave, he saw the girl from the party disappear around a corner on her bike. He looked back to the lake, and the sailboat was gone, somewhere behind the island. It seemed like an omen.

Robert climbed back on the sidewalk and began to walk quickly along the shore, past the heating plant and through the park to West Street. He didn't want to go home yet, and he walked quickly to clear his head, then more slowly when he came to the park, moving in a strange calm under the high branches, past the tall columns of the trees that stood between the courthouse and the lake. A few dry leaves lay on the ground, but most were still holding to their branches.

As he reached the edge of the park, he looked at the bronze figure of a soldier in the uniform of the Canadian Army in the first world war. The arm was raised and the body angled as if the man were running forward, but as Robert moved past it, the figure seemed to be going backward into the trees to lie down in the leaves, not in death, but in a backward motion in which he became a child, his imaginary brother. Robert saw him as two figures, the brother running forward into battle, his arm raised, and the other lost brother who always fell backward through time. He stopped and stared at the figure, black and dramatic against the sky that was as blue as the sky of a postcard.

Robert turned and walked toward his apartment. What he wanted right now was a drink and some food. Later he might read or go to a movie. He would fill the time.

By the time he reached his apartment Robert was very hungry, and he cut himself a piece of camembert to eat while he drank his gin and tonic and cooked supper. He took some beef liver and began to peel and slice onions; by the time he had them in a frying-pan, his drink was finished and he mixed another and began to sip it as he sliced tomatoes and put them in with the onions, then put the liver on to fry in another pan. He remembered that he had some red wine in the bottom of a bottle and he poured it over the liver and covered the pan.

The phone rang. He turned down the heat under the two pans and went to answer it. The voice was Jennifer's, and at first there was pleasure in its familiarity, in his own response to it. Like a key that fitted some lost door. A touch.

"Hello Jenny."

"Do you have a minute?"

And at once the anger. There seemed to be no beginning, no reason, as if it was a response to the very rhythm of her speech. Asking if he was busy, as if his life was full and rewarding and he had no time for her or the children. When was he ever busy?

"Of course."

"Could you manage to take the children Saturday morning as well as the afternoon?"

"Why?"

Mentally Robert took that back, said no to his own impulse, agreed with her and hung up.

"I have some things to do."

He hated the vagueness whenever a man was involved. She patronised him, treated him with care, handled him. As if he were a child. He wanted to kill her.

"Have you told the kids? I don't want them sulking all day because they're stuck with me."

"They always tell me what a good time they've had with you."

"I'm glad they tell someone that."

"If they told you, you wouldn't listen."

"You know all about me, don't you?"

"I didn't phone to argue, Robert."

"But you're willing to join in."

Robert could feel the fury increasing, a pressure in his throat and in the back of his head.

"Can you take them Saturday morning?" Patiently, as to a child.

"Of course." He raged silently.

"Thank you." She hung up.

Robert put down the receiver and stood, with his eyes shut, beating his fist against the wall, screaming inside his head, until the anger wore itself out enough that he could open his eyes and look down at the black shape of the phone on the small table beneath him. Beside it stood the glass with his drink which he now took in his hand and drained, walking to the kitchen and filling it again, the drink stronger this time so that the taste of the gin dominated. He stared at the food cooking in the two pans, then forced himself to turn his attention to it, each gesture consciously made, as if he were acting out this performance of getting supper, eating, drinking, mixing another drink.

By the time he finished, he was beginning to feel drunk, careless. When he stood up from the table he bumped against it and nearly dumped the plate. He walked into the small living-room of the flat and sat down in the armchair without bothering to turn on any lights. There was a little light from the kitchen, and Robert's eyes moved around the room assessing it, weighing it in his mind and finding it without substance.

A wooden bookshelf painted white, with a couple of novels, an anthology of poems, several paperbacks of Freud, some history and biography in paperback. A second-hand rocking chair painted brown with a red cushion on the seat. Molly had bought that for him. A coffee-table with the telephone and a small book of telephone numbers. On the wall an expensive calendar with reproductions of Picasso's drawings. Jennifer had given him that for Christmas.

He wondered if love was nothing more than the euphoria of beginnings, the pain of endings. Or was it a language he had never learned? As his eyes moved around the room, he thought again of Jennifer, and remembered the last time they'd been happy.

The year before they'd moved to Kingston, they'd taken a holiday together, driving a station-wagon through Quebec and around the Gaspé peninsula. It was May, and in Toronto the leaves were out, but as they drove northeast past Montreal and along the south shore of the St. Lawrence, they were driving back into winter. Past Rivière du Loup, they began to see snow still lying on the ground. Neither of them had been through this part of the country before, and they seemed detached and happy, separate from themselves, adventurous. Late in the second day, they were driving along the north coast of Gaspé, the St. Lawrence no longer muddy with tidal silt as it had been farther west, but wide and blue, more like an ocean than a river. They stopped to cook supper on the Coleman stove they'd brought with them, and ate standing up in the chilly wind, looking out over the water. A freighter in the distance looked still, like a toy ship.

They drove on until it seemed close to getting dark, then pulled off the road and parked on a small sideroad that ran a hundred feet and stopped at a snowdrift. Robert opened a bottle of gin, and they cooled their drinks with snow. They were on a hilltop and could see for miles across the water. They stood together to watch darkness come out of the east.

They spread their large sleeping-bag in the back of the station-wagon. By now the air was cold, and they clung together for warmth, then made love, feeling exposed and vulnerable.

In memory they seemed hardly to have spoken that night or in the morning when they woke shortly after sunrise and began to drive through the sleeping towns, then inland over curving and precipitous roads, seeing on each side of them woods still filled with snow, the green of spruce and pine and the red twigs of the birches bright in the sunlight. When they reached the seacoast, they stopped at the top of a hill to make breakfast. Looking east there was nothing between them and Europe but the weight of the Atlantic, and the sharp wind seemed to carry that weight. The grass and trees were bent by it. There were no woods here. Everything was windswept, bleak and shining. Robert remembered a moment when he held a mug of hot tea in his hand and turned to look at Jennifer who squatted behind the car to urinate, her heavy body somehow concentrating all its reality tightly together to strike him more intensely.

As they went along the coast they drove into low cloud, the whole air a kind of pale fog, the sea reflecting the grey silver of the sky. Then out over the sea, a hole opened in the moving clouds and a patch of brilliant silver began to scud over the water, a shining focus to all the white and grey and silver. I am happy, Robert had said to himself. I am a happy man.

They drove on, and somehow it broke as it always did; something fell apart between them, the rhythms became jagged, awkward, until Robert began to wonder if all the hours before had happened only for him, if she had never been part of it.

The road along the south coast of Gaspé was rutted and pocked. The country was poor and ugly. They argued.

I don't want this pain, Jenny. I don't want all my memories to come to this. I will stand up from my chair as if I were a hero. I will walk to the table and pour gin in my glass. I will get drunk, then sleep.

3

Am. Elizabeth waking. Sunlight in the eyes, the body awkward with sense. Morning is. I am. Elizabeth waking. Casting back for the last echoes of the dream, like an odd smell, vanished. There was. There was what, perhaps a face, round, Martha's? Outside the window clear morning sunlight, leaves and branches. Morning is. I am.

She climbed from bed, the long white nightdress dropping out of its bed folds, almost touching the floor as she walked to the stove and put on a kettle of water. Curious clear stream coming from the tap into the metal container. She went to the small bathroom, splashed cold water on her skin, encountered the surprise of her face in the mirror, then walked back into the sunlit bedroom and stood still in its centre, her eyes moving slowly around her, feeling surfaces, saying I am, I am, I am, until it almost seemed that the walls would fall toward her. She stretched and looked upward at her hands that were like strange birds fluttering in the light. She turned slowly, taking the room, taking in the room, feeling the surfaces. I am. I am. I am. Elizabeth. From the closet she took her dark blue dressing gown. Put it on, brushed her long hair. There was a girl in the mirror, with a triangular face and a high forehead, brushing her dark hair. Her hands were like white birds, this girl. Whoever you are.

Elizabeth felt the sudden shiver of fear knowing that she could hate this girl in the mirror, her long face, white birds of hands, that the mirror could freeze them.

Soon the kettle hissed softly, and she went to it, made her cup of coffee and took it to the window ledge. Outside, the street was, for the moment, empty. Grey church, brick houses, leaves lying on the pavement in sunlight. I am. I am. I am. For a few minutes she sat still, looking out. She picked up the *Journal* of Saint-Denys-Garneau and opened it at her bookmark: *Mais puisque de toute façon votre face a chaviré et vous a trahi, on a pensé qu'il serait bon de se dépouiller de cette apparence encombrante et d'être réduit à la simple dureté des os, au silence des os.* The bird in the bone cage; she had begun to shake when she first read that poem, even now the thought of it began a kind of fluttering all through her. She could feel her bones shining. She wished she could write about Garneau, or talk to somebody about him, about the body being contained in the soul, the first of the soul's organizing images, yet she resisted putting words on paper as if they were a secret. It was an image, how could you tell it as a thought?

A light blue Volkswagen turned the corner and moved past her window, driven by a young woman wearing a blazer. Elizabeth's eyes followed the car down the street until it vanished behind the edge of the window frame. She imagined its progress onward, composed for the woman a job, a life.

She lifted the cup, and the hot bitter coffee stung her mouth. I am a tongue. Teeth. A throat. I am. She sipped the coffee again.

The sun was rising higher, shining over her legs under the two layers of cloth, one blue, one white, then skin which was some other white, layered, many skins really. Then flesh. Then bone. *Le silence des os.* She read on through the journal as the sun moved higher, as cars and men and women moved through the street beneath her. She liked to notice familiar people; she was reassured by their recurrence, the same children walking to the same school, the same old women to the same stores. Like a familiar story. The Chinese boy who walked by with his mother just before 9 each day. These things happened, it seemed. These movements took place each day, while within her there were waves and sparks, shimmerings at the edge of transparency, within her windows became mirrors in the play of shadow and again became clear glass. I am a girl sitting in a window, the window of my room which is pale blue and white. I am dressed in a blue dressing-gown that I wear every day at this time because it gives me pleasure. I am reading the notebooks of a poet. Sometimes I must look for a word in the dictionary beside me. *Le silence des os.* I am. I am. I am.

She put out her fingers and touched the glass of the window, which was cool and smooth against her fingertips. She let them rest there just to show herself that she was doing this. This. Like Garneau holding off sleep in order to feel his own presence in willing that.

Her days had such curious shapes now, this empty year. But it was right. The money her grandmother Ross had given her for school had lasted past her graduation, and one day she had thought of this, to spend the year reading or thinking or only sitting in silence with her fingers against the glass of the window.

The last of the children had passed. It must be 9 o'clock. Now they sat in their rows of desks, hands went up, down, pencils and pens moved; she saw it all in primary colours, unshadowed light. It was a world apart.

Now she drew her fingers off the glass and turned the page of the book, a scattering of possible plans for the day moving over the surfaces of her mind, held back from definition, from the terrible lucidity of intention. Almost abruptly she stood up and went to the bed, removed the pillow, began to draw the white sheets toward the top left hand corner, drawing them tight and smooth with her hands, tucking them under the mattress, folding the top one back six inches over the blue wool blanket, moving across the top of the bed to make the other corner smooth and even, picking the pillow up from the floor and fluffing it in her two hands, taking the dark blue cushions from the wicker chair and putting them on the bed, her hands saying this, this.

She put on another kettle of water for coffee, and while she was waiting for it to boil she picked up Martha's letter from its place on the desk, letting her eyes rest on the small square letters, almost without reading.

> *. . . but here I am trapped in the obvious again, that you never see home truly till you've been away—except those people, you, maybe, who are sometimes away even when they're among us. Miss you, miss Sarah. But I don't write to her. It would be the wrong thing. So I need your letters especially much. . . .*

Elizabeth hadn't written for two weeks now. Every day she would pick up Martha's letter and read it, brood over it. She couldn't quite find the words of an answer. Yesterday she had decided to type out pieces of the Garneau notebooks and send those, but somehow that seemed wrong too. Elizabeth remembered Martha's friend Sarah, the edge of excess on Sarah's energy, the echo of falseness. The too-bright collages.

Elizabeth decided to set aside the afternoon to write to Martha. It was the only way, simply to make that decision and do it. She couldn't understand the odd resistance in herself; there had been times when she wrote to Martha twice a week, and she had a deep need for the letters. This block had nothing to do with Martha really, just a silence that had come on herself in the last few weeks, words more and more foreign. What she should do was try to write about Garneau, tell Martha that.

She made her coffee with a series of economical automatic gestures and took it back to the window.

She put down the Garneau notebooks and reached for the volume of his poems.

Mes enfants vous dansez mal. . . she remembered the notes from the journal about the child as metaphysician. She tried to remember her own childhood, but the image of the children in the imaginary classroom, the simple children in primary colours came first. In primary colours and an absolute un-shadowed space.

That passionate curiosity of childhood; looking at the covers of books with the sense that on the other side of those covers was another world. Saw herself small, foreshortened as she looked down from above, from now, a little girl standing in her father's library. It was dim, and there was an odd smell, and she would go there alone and look at the covers of books that contained secrets. Sometimes she felt that she was waiting there for someone to come. If her mother came Elizabeth would be sent away. If her father came he would talk to her and the mystery would recede somehow, go away into the walls ready to come back the next time she was alone. It wasn't her mòther or father she waited for. There was a curious chill somewhere in her bones with the waiting and the sense of the mystery of who she was waiting for. It seemed a little danger-ous to be alone with this feeling, and perhaps her mother knew that and sent her away, outside.

Il faut dire qu'il est difficile de danser ici
Dans ce manque d'air
Ici sans espace qui est toute la danse.

Being there in that room, it had always seemed a little hard to get her breath. As if there was not enough space in the dim light of the room.

Later she had read some of the books out of the sets of Balzac, Dickens, Eliot, held the gold embossed morocco in her hands, but by then the secret had migrated somewhere else, back into the walls of the house or the circuits of the mind or the lost memories.

It was still there, still a secret provoking her curiosity, some-thing that at the beginning of every book was the possible revelation that might reach her by the end. Ideas accumulated in the mind, an area of light expanded and contracted but there was still always something outside it. *Mes enfants, vous dansez mal.*

The last of the coffee, just warm now, slid down her throat. The sun had disappeared behind the clouds and there was a threat of rain in the grey light. Elizabeth crossed to the small bathroom, took off her dressing-gown and night-gown and got into the shower. She turned the nozzle to one side. Even so the first spurt of cold water splashed off the wall and chilled her, but soon the water was warm and comfortable and she moved the soap smoothly over the white skin, still thinking of the bones beneath, feeling her ribs and spine, the tree on which she grew.

It was as she was drying herself that she heard the phone ring. She stepped out into the room, her skin shocked by the air, cold because she wasn't quite dry. It was Burtch on the phone asking her if she wanted to meet him for lunch. As she talked to him, she saw her naked body in the mirror over her dressing table as if she were seeing it through someone else's eyes. There was something almost comic about this naked girl holding a telephone, her face moving in response to the words she spoke and heard, while her body was just there, as arbitrary as the corpse in a murder mystery.

She turned away from the mirror, not wanting to see it. When she had agreed to meet Burtch at a restaurant downtown, she hung up the phone, went quickly to her dresser and took out clothes and put them on. When she went back to her place in the window, she was bored, unable to sit still. The room began to grow close, tight. She must do something, quickly now, quickly. Get outside and more. Walk to the water, cross the water. Take the ferry to the island.

She went to her closet and took out a dark green corduroy jacket and then almost without a stop in the motion of taking it out, putting it on, opening the door, was out the door and running down the steps toward the street. Walked through the sunlight, walking fast through a light wind. This was better. Anyone who watched her would see how happy she was now, to be outdoors like this and with someplace to go.

The old houses, brick, stone, were solid, old, warm. At Palmer's two boys were shouting along the street to each other. Everything moved on these streets or sat where it belonged. And at the foot of the street, the lake, between leaves, shining, glittering. She walked faster. When she reached Ontario Street she saw that the ferry was already at the dock and taking on cars, and she began to run, along the street and down the hill to the pier, out toward the squat black-and-white boat that waited at the edge of the blue water. She felt light and easy running here.

An old man, bald but with reddish hair on his hands and wrists stood at the end of the pier directing cars onto the ferry. He looked toward her as she walked aboard.

"You're pretty quick," he said.

"I didn't want to miss it."

"There's always another one."

Elizabeth walked on board the ferry and up the steep metal stairs to the upper deck. Inside the cabin were two older women with shopping-bags. She went past the cabin door and back to the open deck where she stood in sunlight, the wind moving her hair. There were still a few cars lined up on the pier and a large truck that would be brought on last and parked crossways between the two gangplanks.

From this angle the city looked old and almost noble, the dome of the city hall, the two domes of the Anglican cathedral, the sharp spire of the Roman Catholic cathedral reaching into the clear sky and giving the city a settled, European look. It was like a painting. Things fell into place, had a propriety of place, knew it.

The large truck was brought on board, the gangplank raised, and the engines began to shake the boat. They moved out toward the island, and the city grew small. Moving with the boat, it was like a sleep. Sun and air and a total detachment, moving in light.

Against the rail stood a boy of fourteen or fifteen. His clothes were cheap and old, and his face had a sullen look. He kept his body pressed against the rail. Elizabeth noticed how thin he was, how knotted against the world. He took out a package of cigarettes and turned away from the wind to light one, but the match kept blowing out. He went into the cabin, lit the cigarette and returned to the rail, standing in exactly the same place, his body in the same position.

Elizabeth, entranced by the boat's movement, felt that he had never left. Reality was unreliable. She saw her father, somewhere, was it in her mind? There was a scar beside his nose from an accident years before. Broken glass. The wind blew her hair, her face. Blew across her mind; her eyes were unfocused, seeing light. The boat moved, the city grew small. Gulls. Water. Light.

She and a large gull exchanged a glance, two cold eyes. The gull gave her his eye; everything small. The boat went on, the engines a rhythmic hum in the pit of the stomach.

When the boat landed at Wolfe Island, there were a few cars waiting on the pier, but beyond that the town seemed deserted. Lost in silent light, floating, away from the world. She floated with the boat and the island, the boat turned, they came back to the city, which grew larger again like a painting that grew in the eye and expanded until you were inside, and the flat rhythm of the colours became dimensional, confusing.

The ferry docked again at Kingston, and Elizabeth carried her silence down to the earth and walked slowly along the streets to reach the restaurant where she would meet Burtch.

He wasn't there yet, so she took a place in a booth where she could see the door and drank a cup of coffee. She had almost finished by the time he walked in the door and found her.

She watched him moving toward her in the aisle between the counter and a row of booths. Wearing a suit, he looked to her as if he were in costume, or wearing borrowed clothes. The awkwardness of his heavy body in the brown suit made her feel protective and affectionate. As if she should marry Burtch so he'd have someone to look after him.

His body swayed as he walked along the restaurant, and as a young girl got up from one of the booths, inevitably he bumped into her, then stopped to apologize, his face taking on a look of uneasiness, the dark eyebrows crowding together. When he turned away from his apologies, he saw Elizabeth and waved.

"Hi, beautiful," he said as he slid into the other side of the booth. "How are you doing?"

"Just fine. How's Lawyer Burtch?"

"Not bad. They invited me for dinner last night."

"Was it fun?"

"No. I was concentrating so hard on not spilling my wine that I spilled my coffee. They were very nice about it. They're always very nice about it. That's what I hate."

"Poor Burtch."

"Yeah. That's what I say. I suppose it's what I deserve for trying to become a lawyer. Should have been a butcher like the old man. Got the hands for it."

He laid his fat hands on their backs on the table.

"Just like two little pigs," he said.

Elizabeth smiled, but she did feel somehow repelled by his hands. He was right. They *were* like pigs.

"Tell me about the dinner," she said.

"Well, there he was, Craig Wardell, lawyer, alderman, sharp dresser, in his elegant double-breasted suit with his elegant double-breasted wife. She was wearing a hostess gown. And there I was, trying not to spill my wine. You wouldn't believe how much energy you can use in trying not to spill your wine. I was sweating like mad. Maybe I was sitting too close to the candles. Anyway I nodded and smiled a lot and said 'Yes, that's certainly true,' and as I drank more wine, they got more and more elegant and finally I spilled my coffee."

Elizabeth laughed, looking at the way Burtch drew his features together in a look of rueful concentration. It helped to make the story funny, but it was one of those expressions that seemed to have been adopted because it let him turn everything into a joke. When he looked like that, no-one took him seriously, and he didn't have to take himself seriously.

Once or twice Elizabeth had seen him when his face seemed to have lost all its expressions and become dead flesh. It would stay that way for a few hours, maybe a couple of days, then he would find himself again in some twist of his features, and he would be the same as ever.

"Tell me what you've been up to," he said.

Elizabeth was about to speak when the waitress came to take their order. She was a small girl with thin blond hair, and as she wrote on her pad she chewed the edge of her lip. Burtch ordered sandwiches for them and coffee and the girl moved away to the small kitchen that was at the end of the counter.

"You were just going to tell me the story of your life," he said.

"I haven't been doing much really," she said. "Yesterday afternoon I went for a long ride on my bike, right out Division to Highway 401 then back along Counter Street to Portsmouth and down to the lake, then home along the water. It was so beautiful to be out riding in the sun. By the time I got home, my head felt all funny from the wind and the sun so I lay down on my bed. I fell fast asleep. But I woke up in the middle of the night. I got up and everything was quiet, and I just sat there for a long time listening to it. Then I went back to sleep. And this morning I read."

"The Wardells seem worried that I don't have a girl that I plan to marry on the very day I go into practice. They keep suggesting that if there was anyone I should certainly bring her round."

"You could take me sometime, just to upset their calcula-

43

tions."

"That would make them very excited. Not only a girl, but one who's beautiful and intelligent. But it would be a lie, wouldn't it?"

"It would just be a game."

"Actually I think you'd make them uneasy. They can patronise me because I'm awkward and a bit inept socially, but they couldn't do that to you. It would be strange."

The waitress brought their food, her thin arms looking as if she couldn't manage the tray and would likely drop something. She got everything on the table safely and walked away, still chewing her lip.

Burtch ate half his sandwich and took a drink of his coffee.

"Actually it was last night that I decided that after my six months at Osgoode, I'm going to go back home to practise. I really am a smalltown boy. Even Kingston's too big for me. My Mum and Dad have always wanted me to go back, and I've been hesitating about it, but I'm sure now. It's time to go home and settle down. Sit and smoke cigars and get fat."

It made Elizabeth curiously uneasy to hear Burtch talking about going away. There weren't many people she felt so comfortable with. Burtch accepted her simply, not making demands. Except that one time he'd come to her door, drunk, at three in the morning. He was in a strange mood, angry and demanding, and he had exploded and slapped her, but finally she'd got him to leave, and the next day he wrote her a letter apologizing, and it hadn't happened again.

She remembered how she had felt that night, the cold rigidity that invaded her along with a sense of terrible loneliness. She was alone in the night with a madman, a man who had betrayed her, who raged around her body like a frustrated child, held her by the shoulders and shook her as she became colder and colder, more and more completely passive. When he slapped her it didn't seem to hurt at all. She just let it happen. She was beyond caring.

Remembering that night, she looked at Burtch's face as his jaws moved happily down on the food. He loved to eat. He was right, when he went back to his hometown, he would get fat. He would marry soon after he went there, probably a girl younger than he was. He would make a good husband. As he got older his wit would sharpen, but he would keep it to himself, apearing the same jovial man he'd always been, while within him there hid a cruel sense of the ridiculous.

It was all clear in Elizabeth's mind, as if it were memory. The whole movement was so clear. She saw his wife, children, dog. The cigars. The middle-aged woman who was his secretary. Burtch alone in his office late on a spring afternoon, a happy man.

Elizabeth took her sandwich and began to eat. She wondered if she could be wrong in what she imagined, but it seemed so clear, so sure.

It would happen like that.

"Do you think I'm right?" he said.

"I can just see you, out walking in the country with your dog and your children."

"Have to find a wife first."

"You will."

"I'm not doing so hot."

"You haven't put your mind to it. You waste too much time with me, being my friend and putting up with my foolishness."

"I like that."

"You don't really, Burtch. It's just a habit you've got. It's convenient in a way because it keeps you from having to decide what you really do want. You want me but I won't go beyond some kind of friendship, so you don't have to risk anything anywhere else. You don't have to know who you are."

He drank from his coffee cup without looking at her. Elizabeth felt detached, almost angry with him. She could feel his hurt and it weighed her down, she felt lethargic, bored, wanted to hurt him to get free of that.

"It's just emotional laziness, Burtch, pretending to yourself that you love me. Once you've left here, you'll think of me and be relieved that I'm nowhere near you."

"Well, that's what you think, Lizzie. I think I'll miss you."

"Why?"

"Because being with you makes me happy."

"Or unhappy in a way that you're used to."

"That's cynical."

"What is?"

"To say that happiness is just unhappiness that we're used to."

"But I'm very cynical, Burtch, you know that."

She was flying now, hard and distant.

"There's a saying by La Rochefoucauld that we're never as happy or unhappy as we pretend we are. What we all like best is our familiar habits, even if we call them suffering. And we pretend great melodramas to ease the boredom which is all we really want."

"Do you believe all that?"

"Probably. And that's why I think when you go away and settle down, you'll discover a set of habits that are truer than your old ones. And you'll be relieved."

"You're always very clever, Lizzie."

"Putting me in my place?"

"You could call it that."

"I'll miss you, Burtch. No-one else would put up with so much nonsense from me. Would they?"

"I imagine lots would. Given the chance."

Elizabeth finished her sandwich and drank the rest of her coffee. She didn't want to be alone. Not yet.

"Let's have dessert," she said.

Burtch nodded his head and turned to signal the waitress. Sometime in the last few minutes, the girl had found time to put on lipstick, and the colour on her thin lips made her look sickly. Elizabeth found herself staring at the girl, trying to

46

make her life real. She wore no wedding ring and was very young, but still Elizabeth felt that she had a child. She was sure of it. In a room, no, in an apartment she shared with her mother or her older sister. She saw the room.

Burtch ordered pie and Elizabeth ordered rice pudding. It seemed now that neither of them had anything to say. The air between them was void; they were both turned inward. Elizabeth wished to say something cheerful, but every thought in her mind seemed to fall into darkness. Hands moved. Mouth. Burtch wiped his lips with his napkin.

"I'd better get back soon," he said.

Elizabeth nodded. She picked up the bill that the waitress had left on the edge of the table and worked out how much she owed. She took out the money and gave it to him, and they both stood up. They were tense and silent, and the shape of the moment was wrong. Elizabeth must find the words, however empty, to make it right.

"I'm glad I came out for lunch," she said. "I sit there brooding in my room, and it's great to get out and see somebody."

"Just call me. I have lunch down here every day."

When they reached the street Burtch smiled and waved as he turned and moved awkwardly along the pavement. For a second, Elizabeth watched him walk between the other bodies that crowded this part of the street. She turned and went toward her apartment.

Later she might go for a long ride on the bike, but now she felt uneasy, fragmented, and she wanted to go where she could sort through her memories of the conversation, think of Burtch settled in his new life.

Passing the Christian Science reading-room, she remembered all the times she'd planned to go in, just out of curiosity to be in the strange neat place, but she never had, felt now that she never would. Everything associated with Christian Science was so cleanly. It was intriguing.

She saw again Burtch in his middle age, fat, settled, with his cigar, listening to some story from his children. She wondered if he would ever remember her then.

As she walked up Princess Street, she saw a motorcycle parked at the curb. A man who had black hair and wore the colours of a motorcycle club leaned back against it, with his boots on the edge of the curb. He was talking to two other men who stood leaning against the wall of a building. One of the men was big and bearded and as he looked at Elizabeth approaching, she saw that he had a cast in his eye. It made his face a mask. She was afraid of him. The other two noticed Elizabeth without actually looking at her, and as she walked past they stopped talking so that she felt a kind of ominous silence in which she noticed her own breathing as if it were a conscious action.

Just as she was past, she heard glass breaking and a shout from inside the door of the beer parlour that was beside them. She felt something was about to explode around her or inside her; it didn't, she walked on, and the street was just a street in September sunlight.

As she moved on, the fear and excitement reverberated inside her, the moment's tension led on into fantasies, the three men armed with knives, chains, the street going dim as the fantasies opened like flowers in her mind. She reached the door of her house. The Victorian stained-glass window was brilliant in the afternoon sun. A young knight, features as delicate as a girl's, stood in his armour at the centre of a pattern of blue and green and gold glass. He held a shield in his left hand and a sword pointed upward in his right. He seemed too delicate to fight, as if he must be the one whose blood would be spilled. She remembered the odd, uneven eyes of the big man beside the motorcycle. She saw herself in those eyes, bleeding, hurt.

Walking up the stairs, she felt the solidity of the steps as a surprise, for she was aware of the planet's whirling in space, of herself only as a loose fragment.

Once inside her room, she stood still for a moment, then

48

began to undress, hanging the blouse in the closet, folding the jeans and putting them away in a drawer. Her hands moved by themselves, detached from her. Her hands. The slim hands of the knight. The hard hands of the men, grease worked into the skin. A hand holding a knife.

She glanced at Martha's letter on the desk. Saw Martha's face, round, still, solid. She took off the last of her clothes and put on the long dressing-gown, then walked through the room, feeling it move around her, feeling herself hidden within it.

She lay down on the bed, on her back, perfectly still. The young knight lay bleeding, the mark of a knife on his white soft skin. Men stood around him. Their knives were marked with his blood and they wiped them clean on the hard greasy denim of their trousers. They wore black, their hair tangled, and they were silent.

Elizabeth felt the hands move over her skin. It tingled with awareness. This. This. She lay absolutely still, absolutely still. Her hands moved over the nipples. The knight lay at an awkward angle and there was a purple cloth laid across his body and the blood that poured from his belly began to soak into the cloth. Their eyes turned to her, hard. One lit a cigarette and drew in deeply, his lips working around it. They didn't put the knives away, but moved toward her and as she looked at them they were above her, faces black, teeth. Her hands lay still beside her, waiting, waiting. She lay on the bed, her white skin shining.

4

Robert glanced through the Potterton manuscript, starting with the last chapter and moving forward, looking at each chapter then putting it down, trying to get clear in his mind the strengths and weaknesses of the book's structure. It seemed to him that there was some kind of hole somewhere, that something was missing that would make the argument solid and convincing, but he hadn't been able to get his hands on it.

He thought of the discussion he'd had with Wilson about it the night he'd gone to dinner. It had been a splendid dinner, beef and kidney pie and good wine, but Robert had found himself nervous. Being there alone like a young bachelor made him uneasy. He didn't want to observe a happy marriage, and Wilson's marriage did appear to be one that satisfied both partners. There was a kind of gentle teasing that went on between him and Edith that suggested real and lasting affection. Robert envied it, but knew it as something that wasn't possible for him. Sitting at the table with brandy, listening to Wilson talk about the book, Robert had felt misplaced, inadequate.

The book itself was intriguing, a study of the way in which the development of a commercial empire was reflected in British popular culture, but Robert knew little of the source material and little of the economic history so that he found himself, at times, dealing with the book in a way that was simply picayune, brooding over punctuation. Wilson was enthusiastic about the book, or as enthusiastic as he allowed himself to be, but the academic experts had been less completely in agreement than they had hoped. At dinner, Robert had simply sat nodding agreement, but now he thought he was on the track of an important flaw in the way the book was put together. He felt he might be able to get it sorted out if he could decide why the argument seemed to miss a step somewhere.

Robert leaned back in his chair and stared at the ceiling. Entered, shining, Ray Statler: orange shirt, red and black tie, black trousers.

"You like like a Baltimore Oriole," Robert said.

"Better than looking like a domestic shit-pigeon like everyone else around here. What are you up to?"

"On the track of a structural flaw. Like a bloodhound. I

think I'm about to do something useful."

"How come you're so cheerful today?"

"My time of the month. The moon is full."

"Margita says she can always tell if it's a full moon. Got me up out of bed last night to go and look. So then I stayed up and drew this great picture of her and the moon."

"Funny to think of women being on the same cycle as the moon. I read something about the astrologers and scientists starting to agree with each other about moon cycles."

"For a while I had this idea for an astrological calendar of drawings. My old girlfriend was very big on astrology. Wouldn't fuck anyone unless their stars were right."

"That must have been awkward."

"I don't know. She said my stars were right. But how would I know? I don't give a shit about anything unless I can use it."

Something clicked in Robert's mind about the arrangement of material in chapters.

"Beat it Ray," he said. "I've got an idea."

Ray smiled and made an obscene gesture as he left. Robert took out three chapters of the book and began to summarize the material in them. Within an hour he had the problem solved. It would need another few pages, another set of examples from literature after 1780, but it would work. Wilson was away for the afternoon, so Robert wrote a note explaining what he'd worked out, clipped it to the front of the manuscript and left it on Wilson's desk. It was a bit early but he decided to leave the office and walk home. He was taking Gavin and Cindy out to dinner so he'd walk home now and pick up his car in lots of time to wash and meet them.

It was another bright day, the air suggesting the coolness of autumn, the leaves beginning to turn, and he walked along the street with great pleasure. When he reached the corner, he was about to cross when he saw the girl from the party passing on her bicycle. He waved to her, and she waved and pulled over to the curb. She was wearing a short tweed skirt, and her calves were long and smooth.

"Hi," she said. "I was thinking about you today." She had bright teeth, bright eyes, an odd mouth and jaw.

"What were you thinking?"

"Just wondering where you were and what you were doing."

"Sitting behind a desk in a little brick house down the street and thinking about a manuscript."

"Did you think anything interesting?"

"Yes. I was very clever today. What have you been up to?"

"Mostly sitting in my little room."

"Not going to classes?"

"I'm not a student. I graduated last year, but I had some money left over that my Grandmother Ross gave me to go to school, so I decided I'd just sit and read and think."

"Don't you get bored?"

"Sometimes. Then I go for a ride on my bike."

There was a pause. Robert didn't want her to leave. Words began to form. Against his better judgment.

"Are you busy later tonight?" he said.

She shook her head, a curious, almost apprehensive look on her face.

"Could we go out for a drink later on?"

"That would be great." She began to climb back on her bike.

"Sure. But I don't know your name."

Her face took on an expression that seemed to mix embarrassment with mischief.

"Good."

She rode away, turning once to wave at him. Robert walked off smiling absurdly. He'd known that it needed a woman to make him feel alive again, but he had resisted it a long time now. Too long. He remembered the night of the party, her story of the abortion, her frigidity, and speculated on whether he was enrolling for a new course in pain and irritation. What else to do? You couldn't stay dead. He walked home happy, smelling with pleasure every scent that was on the air.

It was still half an hour till the time he'd arranged to pick up the children; he thought of mixing a drink, but instead took a shower and changed his clothes. He put on a dark blue shirt that he'd always been fond of, a woven tie that Cindy had given him for Christmas. To anticipate the evening with pleasure was good, healthy, sane. He had spent too many months closed in behind doors and windows like an invalid.

Pay homage to simple pleasures. While I am not a handsome man, neither am I an ugly one, and there is no harm in paying, for once, a little attention to my clothing. I once did.

He drove to Jennifer's house and honked the horn. He always avoided going in if he could. Figures appeared at the door. Out of memory into light. Gavin ran down the path, Cindy following more sedately. With style. She had class, his daughter. It was good to see that in the way she moved her honey-coloured hair. It was better to be beautiful than not.

"Hi Dad," Gavin said as he climbed in. Cindy smiled and didn't say anything.

"Hi Gavin. Hello Miss Lucinda."

Cindy looked a bit embarrassed.

"Can we get back by 6.30?" Gavin said. "There's a TV program I want to watch."

"Perhaps," Robert said.

Odd how parents thought they were important to their children. Most kids would trade in a father for a TV program or a baseball game or a high-school dance. A good thing, but it angered him sometimes. He could have no influence on them if he wasn't in their lives. Though he might have been a bad or debatable influence when he was. He was often as intolerant with his own children as his father had been with him. His father whom he now avoided seeing.

"Where do you want to go for supper?" he said.

They named different places. Gavin wanted pizza and Cindy wanted Chinese food. He stopped the car to flip a coin. Chinese won.

"She always gets her way," Gavin said. "Spoiled brat."

"Talk about spoiled," Cindy said. "Mother never says a word to you about anything. Little creep."

"Cut it out now," Robert said. "You can be pleasant to each other for an hour or so."

He found himself wondering about what Cindy had said. Was Gavin getting away with too much? He was a strong-willed boy, and he wondered if Jennifer, without a man in the house, gave him too much freedom. He was a cunning little beggar when he wanted something.

"What are you doing in school these days, Gavin?" he said. Ask the obvious question. You may avoid the harder ones.

"Not much. I'm pretty good at fractions."

"Good."

"Hey Dad."

"Yeah."

"Want to hear a fast joke?"

"Sure."

"Want to hear another one?"

Robert snorted with laughter. He'd been taken completely off guard.

"That's an old joke," Cindy said.

"It made me laugh."

He glanced across at Cindy, at her face, which seemed a little sulky, inscrutable, mysterious. Remembered himself at that age, playing baseball in the school yard until dark. He was a person even then, observing, willing, suffering. He remembered once when she was eight, Cindy had explained that she couldn't think of herself as someone who would be older and bigger. She just knew herself from inside, as Cindy, not as a real person. In that same conversation, she had explained to him that it was hard to think of nothing. Even at eight she possessed some kind of perception of mystery. Who was she now? What countries did she inhabit? His child, she was not anyone's. Lucinda, child of light.

54

"What have you been up to, Cindy?"

"Nothing."

"Nothing at all?"

"Same old things."

"How's school?"

"Pretty good. I might be in a play."

"What's the play?"

"It's called *Sally's Dream*. I don't like it much, but I wouldn't mind being in it. There's one good part, a witch."

"Is that the one you want?"

She nodded. Robert was near the restaurant. He found a parking place in the lot behind city hall where the open-air market was just closing. Only two or three booths were still operating, a few baskets of vegetables and bushels of apples sitting beside the roadway.

"Do you want to go to the market and get some apples to take home?" Robert said.

"Mummy just bought some," Cindy said. "She brought them home at noon. But only one basket. We could probably use another."

She was being polite to him. It was touching and painful.

"One basket is probably enough," he said. They entered the restaurant and found a booth. The boy and girl didn't want to sit together so there was a delay while they got themselves into place, the pretty young Chinese waitress standing patiently beside them till they were done. Gavin ordered a hamburger, and Robert and Cindy Chinese food.

As they waited for the food to arrive, Robert watched, through the restaurant window, one of the men at the market loading apples in the back of his half-ton truck, getting ready to leave. The sun was very low now, and the market square was shaded by the buildings on King Street. There was a richness of indirect light. The man was young, small, with short but unruly hair; he didn't look like someone who had spent his whole life on a farm, and Robert found himself wondering if the man had left some other life in a city to become a fruit grower. How did he learn? He had a child with him, a boy of eight or ten. Why wasn't the boy in school?

Gavin was chattering about a school project on airplanes. Cindy listened disdainfully.

"Would you like to be a pilot?" Robert said.

"No. I'm too scared of falling."

"Me too."

Always during these short meetings with his children, Robert found himself searching for significance of some kind, something to make him feel close to them, feel the bond was important, but significance took time, more time than he had. It was a matter of the accumulation of insignificant moments. He remembered walking the floor with Cindy when she was still a baby. She had measles and a high fever, and Jennifer had been up with her for hours. Finally she asked him to take a turn. He remembered the feeling of the child's hot body against his own, her weight in his arms; in that dark hour something had passed between them, but it was perhaps only an impersonal human contact. He could have been any man, she could have been any sick child. There was no magic to parenthood. When he left, he became unimportant.

Against this thought, he talked as he ate, played at being their father in the absence of any necessity for him in that role. When they had finished eating, he drove them to a local dairy for ice-cream cones. And drove them home, the interlude over, pleasant but somehow pointless, conventional. He should have a house they could come to, live in, a life they could join.

The car arrived in front of the house. He hadn't touched either one of them. He reached out and ruffled Gavin's hair.

"See you soon," he said. "Phone me sometime." He could see Jennifer standing at the living-room window. She had no business watching him like this.

"Bye Cindy."

They spoke, were gone. He drove away quickly, not to see

them. He remembered Jennifer in a hospital bed holding Gavin, new born, in her arms. Her breasts huge with milk.

It was too early to call on the girl, so he drove home and sat down with a murder mystery. He didn't want to read anything that required concentration. The thought came that he never did, that what mind he had once possessed had vanished years before.

Not true, not quite true.

Robert read about half the book, stopping around nine. He wondered about driving to the girl's house, but decided to walk and set off through the cool autumn air. The night was clear, with thousands of stars, and Robert walked quickly, breathing deeply and feeling with pleasure the air in his lungs, pleased that he'd made the effort to stop smoking a couple of years before.

He reached the girl's house and stopped to look at the mail-boxes and find out her name. Elizabeth Ross. It was written there in a rather precise script. He went up and knocked on her door.

"Queen Elizabeth," he said as she opened it.

"Robert Dudley," she said, and it took him a second to catch up.

"You're very quick."

"I used to read a lot of historical novels. The romantic sort."

"Are you ready?" he said.

"Just a second." She went to a closet and took out a green corduroy jacket. It emphasized her height. She was very attractive. Robert didn't want to take her to the Plaza or someplace where they might meet friends of hers or his.

"How about the Holiday Inn," he said. "We can admire the view."

"Sure," she said. "I've never been there. I don't drink much."

"The bar's on the top floor with windows looking out over the water."

"That sounds nice."

"I didn't bring my car," he said. "I thought it was too nice a night. You can tell me about the stars."

They walked, and she pointed out stars and constellations. Even when he was shown them, Robert soon lost them again in the chaos of points of light. He liked the names, but didn't care where they stood. But he loved the names, Aldebaran, Polaris, Betelgeuse, Antares. Points of light in darkness, co-ordinates in the endless sea of space.

The bar at the Holiday Inn was beginning to get crowded, but they were lucky and got a table at the window just as it was being vacated. Elizabeth ordered sherry and Robert ordered gin and tonic. When the drinks came, Robert sipped his and leaned back in his chair looking out the window into the darkness and across the water.

The room was full of respectable older couples who seemed to be part of a convention, and at one end of the room was a piano player to entertain them.

The piano player was part of the price you paid for the view. He smiled a lot in an embarrassed kind of way and made a specialty of rippling arpeggios. Sometimes he sang in an in-gratiating whine. Robert imagined him shipped all over North America from one Holiday Inn to another, inviting conventions of tool-and-die salesmen to join in the same songs that had been joined in on by sanitary engineers and graduates of hotel-management courses.

Across the water, Robert could see the lights of the military college. Once, driven inside by Wilson who had a message there, he had sat in the car and watched uniformed cadets marching singly or in pairs across the quadrangle. You went behind those gates and it was a different world, simple, defined. Or you came into the bar of the Holiday Inn and you were in another world. He envied the old woman who sat near the piano player, waving her hands in time to the music and lean-ing over to talk to him between numbers while her husband smiled benignly behind his glasses. It was the envy he always

58

felt for anyone who was not himself, who was unlike him. It was a longing for freedom, not to be trapped within the boundaries of his own personality, not to know how he would respond.

He watched Elizabeth lift the glass of sherry to her mouth and sip it. What, he wondered, was the source of the elegance with which she did it? Did she watch herself in mirrors?

"Do you like this place?" he said.

"I like the feeling of being up in the air, seeing everything way down below far away from me. It's like flying."

"The piano player annoys me."

"He has a good time," she said.

"I wonder what he does all day when he isn't playing here. Maybe they hang him in a closet with a wet rag wrapped around his smile."

"Poor man. He probably comes up here in the daytime when it's empty except for the cleaning woman and plays Bach and Mozart and pretends that he's better than he is."

"It would be hard to pretend to be worse."

"He's making everybody here happy except you. Don't be hard on him."

"I'm hard on everyone. It's just my way."

"Will you be hard on me?" She said it looking at him directly, her eyes holding his.

"Of course."

"Poor me."

Robert was caught in the space between their eyes. He reached for his drink, looked away from her. He wanted this to happen. He didn't want this to happen. Far below, lights were reflected in the water. The piano player had started "Down by the Old Mill Stream" and the crowd was joining in. They were all couples, older than he was, and Robert found himself wondering where they had all learned the song. Singing in the family car on the way home from a picnic in 1933, someone adding the harmony in a quavering tenor. The piano player nodded and smiled.

59

Robert looked at Elizabeth's rather broad bony hands on the table. Her fingernails were cut short. His eyes moved over her body, the long pale neck beside the dark hair; the wide mouth turning down at the corners. He reached out and put the tips of his fingers on the back of her hands. She looked at him, with that curious concentrated stare that still unsettled him.

"Do you think you're pretty?" he said.

"No. I look all right. I don't mind the way I look, but I don't think I'm pretty."

"Are you happy?" Did he really want to know, or was it a ritual, just another approach? Are you happy? Shall we dance? Let's go to bed.

"Right now I feel just fine," she said, looking as if she was about to laugh. "You ask funny questions."

"I don't know you well enough to know what we should talk about. It's better to ask questions and find things out."

"Do you want to know my age and height and weight?"

She was mocking him, and he restrained the urge to say something cruel. He tried to smile.

"Write them on a piece of paper and slip it across the table to me."

"Lend me your pen."

He reached it over to her. She turned over a coaster, wrote on the back of it, folded it and passed it across the table. Robert opened it and held it toward the light. It contained a sentence in French.

La passion ne peut être belle sans excès.

"Who said that?" he said

" Pascal."

"Do you read French?"

"Je l'étudiais pendant quelques années."

It suited her mouth, that language, made it softer and more mobile.

"You have a good accent," he said.

"It's not really."

"Do you believe that?" Robert said, indicating the piece of paper in his hand.

"I don't know. Probably in a way. In books anyway."

"Who do you like besides Pascal?"

"Racine, Baudelaire."

"All the Jansenists."

"I suppose."

"Is that how you live your life?"

"Jansenism?"

"Intensity. Excess. Suffering."

"Only in my dreams."

An image returned to Robert's mind from a dream the night before; it was a landscape, flat and open but with trees and a house in the distance. The trees were all a brilliant autumnal red, scarlet. He was moving toward the house. What had happened inside the house? He couldn't remember. There were people in a group, asking him questions.

"How long have you been in Kingston?" she was asking him.

"Two years. Before that I was in Toronto and England."

To stand up from the table, take her hand, find a cab, a train, a plane, wake in England; Newens for lunch, the Vermeers in the National Gallery, a walk on Hampstead Heath. I imagine gestures too large and cannot reach them, relapse into silence.

"I loved England," Robert said. "In a way I wanted to stay there."

"Why did you come back?"

"I was offered a good job."

"Here."

"No. In Toronto."

"Before I went there, I always imagined England from novels. I could see all the parts but I didn't know how they fitted together. I could see these beautiful little villages with women in long dresses, and I could see London slums and cosy

61

little cottages, but they all seemed to be separate, like a lot of separate dreams that you dreamed at different times but you know they belong together. Do you know what I mean? When I went there I felt as if I was going to turn some special corner and be inside *David Copperfield*. I guess that's what happens when you read too many books and don't know enough about anything else. When I was younger, I read all the time. I loved Dickens and George Eliot."

The words poured out of her, excited, electric, and Robert could feel himself being roused, his energy reaching out to hers. They were far above the ground. Below there was water and light on water. She was watching him intently.

"England's comfortable," he said, "the right size for living in. Like all islands."

"Islands are magic. I used to dream of being like Robinson Crusoe, on an island alone, making my clothes and growing my food. And one day I'd find a boy on the island, like a brother but better. We'd build a house and be king and queen of the island."

Robert was watching her mouth, desire for her coming over him in waves that left him breathless. Yet she seemed a child, seemed to maintain a child's panic and excitement in a voice that was a woman's. It was unbearably hard not to touch her but he didn't want to frighten her. Robert knew now that he would make love to her, but not when. It pleased him to know he could let her find her way to it.

He signaled the waitress to bring another round of drinks. He felt that he was smiling, remembered his success with the manuscript in the afternoon. It was good to be here high in the air looking down. He turned and watched the lights of cars crossing the bridge over the Cataraqui, turned the other way and looked out toward the lights of Wolfe Island.

"I've always loved the idea of Scotland too," she said. "Have you ever been there?"

"Once on holidays."

"That's where my mother's family came from. My grandmother used to talk about Scottish history and the stories her father had told her. When I went to visit her, Scotland used to be more real to me than Canada. I thought everyone in Scotland was a Presbyterian because she was. It was a real shock when I discovered how many of the Highlanders were Catholics. It changed my whole idea of Scotland."

Robert paid for the drinks and lifted his own to his mouth. The piano player had started playing a series of songs by Cole Porter and Rogers and Hart and George Gershwin. He played them almost well, concentrating more of his attention on the piano and less on the audience. Inside him there *was* a musician.

"Listen," he said, "the piano player has started to play real music. Maybe you were right about him."

In the far corner a balding fat man in a brown suit was standing waving his arms in time to the music. Two tables away, his friends laughed and shouted at him. Robert watched as if it were a play being staged for his amusement. The standing man's wife smiled but looked worried, too sober to be at ease with his performance.

So long as Robert looked in that direction, he was an audience, invisible, but when he turned back to the girl, he became visible in her eyes, saw himself performing in her imagination. Wondered how she saw him, or if she saw him at all.

"You look puzzled," she said.

"I guess that's what I was feeling."

"I often get confused when I'm with people, as if they know how things are supposed to go and I don't. I do in a way, but the things that other people say that sound natural to them seem to sound silly when I say them. For a while I had the feeling that there was some kind of secret that I wasn't in on. In high school I always felt that way, that there was something nobody would tell me, but I didn't know what it was. I felt like some kind of a monster. I tried to learn all the right things, but never felt as if they worked."

"In a way you probably had a kind of special gift. Enough imagination to see that things could be different. You could see more alternatives than other people." He was flattering her, yet he believed what he said or wanted to believe it.

"Maybe, but having something extra is the same as having something missing. It means you're not the same shape as other people, your feelings aren't the same."

"Does that bother you?"

"Not much any more. I've learned to be more like what I'm supposed to be."

"Do you like it better that way?"

"Yes. Probably every young girl goes through a strange period. A lot anyway. Maybe I'm glad when the strangeness comes back. I'm not sure."

The piano player had started a series of sentimental Irish songs and the audience was joining him again.

We are here together and sing. The alcohol makes us free and beautiful.

Robert looked at Elizabeth's small breasts, wanting them, wanting her beneath him. Their eyes met, her eyes holding him. Why was he always the first to look away? If he looked at her any longer he would have to touch her. The pressure of her eyes was unbearable. They were locked into some zone of silence in the noisy room, and there wasn't enough air to breathe.

Lift your glass, drink.

The singing ended and the pianist stood up to take a break. He walked to the bar and sat down in a chair beside it. One of the waitresses got him a glass of something.

"Shall we drink up and go?" Robert said.

She nodded and took her glass in her hand. She took one mouthful, and seeing that Robert's glass was empty, stood up.

"I'll wait till you finish," he said.

"I don't really want it," she said.

They walked out of the bar and stood waiting for the

elevator.

When it arrived a dark, handsome young man with big shoulders and sharp clothes got out, holding the door for the expensive blonde who was with him. They looked out of place in Kingston, a bit too rich, a bit too smartly dressed. They were big-city people. The woman was older than Elizabeth, perhaps less attractive, but there was a kind of consciousness in her beauty, her manner. It was all chosen.

They were silent in the elevator and crossing the lobby. When they got outside, Elizabeth breathed deeply.

"It smells clean," she said. "I love the fall."

"Someday we should go for a drive out in the country."

"That's a good idea."

They walked up Princess Street, hardly talking, turning at Wellington to go through the old part of the city. Robert remembered the night in August when they had walked here and decided that this one would not end awkwardly. They turned a corner, and Robert found they were approaching the apartment where Molly and Andrew had lived; in such a small city, you couldn't avoid the past, it was all around you, waiting for you to trip on it or meet it face to face.

He wondered if Molly would be happy with her husband and her baby, or if her discontent would come back sometime in the future. And Andrew. A quiet, cheerful, hidden man who would never show his pain, too much in need of independence to let Molly into his life. He simply shut his mouth and went his way. He had great dignity and Robert had always respected him, even while taking his wife from him. Sir, you are a most noble cuckold. In fact if he could have hated Andrew it might have helped him stay with Molly. There was nothing like a common enemy to weld you together.

"You're very quiet," Elizabeth said.

"Just thinking," he said.

"What about?"

"Old friends. They used to live around here."

"I love this part of the city. It's such a funny mixture of students and rich people and poor people. I sit in my window and watch people going by, and I start to feel that I know them all. There's a little Chinese boy that goes past to school every day, sometimes with his mother and sometimes his grandmother. He's too big to need anyone to take him to school so he looks very strange and sulky. But I see them go by every day and wonder about them. I suppose in a way I like seeing people better than knowing them. If I know them they start to challenge me."

They walked the last block to her apartment.

"Do you want to come in and have tea?"

Robert didn't want to be alone. He wanted company, he wanted to touch her.

"Not tonight," he said. "Maybe some other time."

I will not risk what happiness I have, rather hold it, hoard it, kiss one finger and touch it to the tip of your nose, wave and walk away to my own place which is barren but safe. Walk, walk on, not looking back.

5

The phone rang.

Outside her window was a branch of leaves that was yellow and brilliant red, here and there still green. There was a little wind, and the leaves shivered like nerves moving under the skin of sunlight.

The phone rang. Loudly. Again.

She took the black telephone in her hand. Spoke.

"Hi Lizzie." Burtch's voice. "What are you up to?"

"Nothing. Just lying here daydreaming."

"Have you heard the news?"

"What?"

66

"The FLQ have kidnapped some British diplomat."

The words meant nothing to her.

"Why did they do that?"

"Nobody seems to know yet. Ransom or publicity or both I guess."

"You sound so worried, Burtch."

"I don't like it. Things aren't that bad in Quebec."

"There are crazy people everywhere."

"I suppose."

Elizabeth could imagine his face wrinkled with worry and uneasiness.

"I don't like it, all that kind of stuff."

"I know. Poor Burtch."

"How about having dinner with me tonight?" Burtch said.

"I can't Burtch."

"Anyone I know?"

"No."

"You're being secretive."

"I don't think so."

"Tell me who."

"No. Burtch, don't be so curious."

"I can't help it. The more secretive you are, the more curious I get."

"Well don't. I'm a secretive young girl, so don't poke at me."

"All right," he said grudgingly, "but I thought I was your friend."

"You are, don't get all sulky and childish."

"I do, don't I?"

"Now and then."

"You know how I feel about you, Lizzie."

"I think you exaggerate sometimes."

"I don't think so."

"Don't be mad at me. I need you to be my friend."

"Always am Lizzie. I'm glad if something important is happening for you. I better go. How about lunch tomorrow?"

"Probably. Can you give me a call in the morning?"

"Okay. Have a good time tonight."

"Thanks Burtch."

Elizabeth hung up the phone. She felt trapped; everything was wrong, out of rhythm. The call from Burtch, his jealousy, had somehow made the dinner with Robert more serious, and she didn't want that; she wanted nothing serious, just to go out and have fun and come back. Nothing serious.

She had met Robert in the park the day before, by accident, and they had laughed together in the arched space under the trees. He had asked her out for dinner because they laughed together. That was all there was to it. She didn't want Robert to ask her for anything, to touch her, change things.

Everything was fine while it was simple. With Tom it was that way, but it had changed, and she had lost everything. She remembered a day at the cottage when they were left alone for a few hours and lay side by side on her bed until Tom had grown angry at her refusals, and she had accepted him for the first time and then regretted it.

They sat on the dock at dark, Tom pleased, Elizabeth sad and disappointed. Always at that hour the sun made the sky brilliant red, the fish would begin to jump. She had hidden the stained sheet; she would take it into the woods and bury it, and no-one would ever really miss it. They always lost things at the cottage.

On the desk beside her was a letter from her mother asking if Elizabeth was coming home for Thanksgiving weekend, worrying because she didn't have a job or any clear plans. Her mother was very sensitive to her. The letter seemed almost to know that she was seeing someone new.

Elizabeth thought about Robert's wife; she had never seen her, but she had a sense of her as a tiny quiet woman, rather nervous but very sensitive. Everything was too close, too insistent. The woman would not leave her mind. She put on the kettle to make coffee and took out her copy of *The Mill on the*

Floss, to lose herself in that comfortable world of Maggie Tulliver's childhood. She sat in the wicker rocker so that the sun fell on her feet, and now and then she would look down at them, at their curious shape as the sun illuminated them. They were like those fish that lived in caves and were white and blind.

Kidnap was a funny word. She looked it up in the dictionary, which said it came from *kid* and a variation of *nab*. Kidnabbers. What was it in French? Her dictionary gave *enlever de vive force*; there must be a colloquialism, at least in Quebec. Kidnab. It sounded like a dance. *Mes enfants vous dansez mal*.

She made herself coffee and a peanut-butter sandwich and settled down to read the afternoon away, leaning back in the rocker and letting Maggie Tulliver's world become more real than her own, remembering now and then the first time she had read the book at fourteen, and how she had cried over sections of it. Poor unhappy Maggie.

Late in the afternoon, something began to shape itself in her mind, and she went to her desk and wrote a long letter to Martha. She had received no answer yet to her letter of the week before, but now that she had started writing letters again it didn't matter when she got the answers. She knew how Martha would react to what she was saying, or at least trusted her not to misunderstand it. The letter was almost like a poem, with Maggie Tulliver and the fish in caves both in it. Everything that had moved through her mind except the phone call from Burtch. That seemed to have no place.

The letter went on for nearly twenty pages. When she reached the end and looked up, Elizabeth discovered that it had started to rain. It was nearly time for Robert to pick her up. She folded the letter without rereading it and put it in an envelope. She had no stamps, so sealed and addressed the envelope and left it on her desk.

She had just finished washing and dressing when Robert knocked. When she opened the door, he looked uneasy. He was wearing a checked jacket instead of the heavy cardigans he usually wore.

"You're dressed up," she said.

"A bit. Are you ready?"

"Guess so."

"I brought the car tonight," he said, "in honour of the rain." He laughed, nervously.

"This afternoon I was writing a letter, and I didn't even notice that the rain had started. Sometimes I get so concentrated on what I'm doing that I'm out of touch. It always made my mother furious."

There was something about Robert that made her talk like that, the words out of control. They went out the door and down the street to his car, an American fastback that was bigger than she would have expected.

"This is the last leftover from my career as a publishing executive. When this wears out I'll fold myself into a Volkswagen."

Elizabeth sat down in the front seat, and he closed the door behind her. Robert went round and got in the other side. She felt strange sitting in the car with him, almost as if she had made some kind of commitment. It was different from being in her room or a public place, and she felt subdued, as if it were her place to sit and wait until she was spoken to.

They drove a few blocks to Princess Street and parked in a lot behind one of the Italian restaurants.

The rain was heavier now, and they ran from the car to the door of the restaurant. A sudden shift: from the false composure of the car to a mockery of freedom; they were children running in the rain. Scuttled into shelter. Elizabeth shook the water from her hair. Robert smiled. The gestures seemed to repeat themselves as if in a sequence of mirrors. Elizabeth shook the water from her hair. Robert smiled. They were somewhere inside as if inside a book, defined. Suddenly now, every moment was taking on a shape that was irrefutable.

They would go now and sit at a table, they would be two people sitting at a table and the words would come out of that.

On the walls were badly drawn, mildly obscene illustrations of the voyages of Marco Polo, a Chinese woman with holes cut in her dress so that the nipples showed through, sentences of narrative loaded with heavy-handed *double entendres*. Robert ordered a drink, she didn't want one.

"I don't really drink much."

They faced each other over the table. He would look toward her and then away, avoiding the moment.

We sit in our places, one on each side of the table, man and woman face to face.

They looked at the menu. Elizabeth didn't know whether or not she was hungry. Everything in her was too busy now, but she chose something and waited for it to come.

"What are you reading these days?"

"*The Mill on the Floss.* I've read it a couple of times before, but I felt like reading it again. Then I wrote a twenty-page letter to a friend of mine who's in England."

"Twenty pages?"

"When I sat down everything that was going on in my head just started to think itself out on paper. She's someone I've known for years. She knows me better than anyone else in the world. I always know that she'll understand what I mean, in a way that other people never can."

"It must be nice to have someone that close. I envy you."

"Haven't you ever had a friend like that?"

"No. It may be my own fault. I've always kept people at a distance, men anyway. I find it easier to talk to women. But you can't really be friends with a woman."

"Why not? It should be possible."

"It just doesn't work. I could tell you a dozen stories."

Elizabeth thought of her telephone conversation with Burtch. Felt that the moment of her realization had edges, sharp points. They sat on each side of the table, facing each other, as if they

71

had sat there forever. The waitress brought their food and the moment seemed pleased to find them there together. Their eyes moved, met, moved. Outside it was raining. They sat together at the table, ate.

"Did you hear about the kidnapping?" he said.

She nodded.

"What do you think about it?"

"It isn't real to me. It's just a story that someone told me. I don't read the newspapers. Nothing in them ever seems real."

"But those things may affect your life in dozens of ways that you only half notice."

"Maybe. It doesn't feel that way to me. What I read in the newspaper is just words."

"If you don't have words you'll be using someone else's. You don't exist unless you can say who you are."

"Someone who's sitting at a table with you, eating."

Their eyes met. Something came open in her head, and she felt a flowing down through her spine, along with a curious, carefree sensation all through her limbs.

"You have strange eyes," she said.

"How are they strange?"

"They somehow go into hiding, then when I don't expect it, they show something. I can feel them start to reach me, then all of a sudden they'll disappear again. They're very careful and tentative."

He looked at her, waiting.

"Everyone wants to be recognized," he said.

Elizabeth felt careless.

"Do your eyes ever get carried away?" she said.

"Sometimes. But then it always seems to fail."

"Is that what happened to your marriage?"

He did it then, vanished from his face, and yet she could still feel some kind of force coming from him into the air, making it hard for her to breathe.

"I guess the answer to that would depend who you asked."

"You."

He was looking down at his long hands that were spread on the table in front of him. She wanted to touch the hands, see if he would pull them away. It was odd, this pouring out of feeling, so confident.

"My wife would say that I was childish, unstable. That my needs were too intense, and that I always blamed someone else for what went wrong. That I was self-indulgent, lacked any real concern about my children, certainly had no real feeling for her, that I used my intelligence and whatever insight I might have had to try and destroy her or imprison her inside my fantasies. That's what my wife would say."

He stopped and looked across the table. It was like rocking in a high wind. There was a curious trembling across her shoulders, and the sense of freedom was almost lost. When she met his eyes, she felt as if she were testing herself, trying to have the strength to win it back, his eyes met hers, yet were withheld.

"You *are* very intense," she said.

"As are you. You're electric, as if you were the focus of a huge field of energy. It's frightening."

The field of energy now included him, was drawing him toward her to touch her. That she must touch him, the slender hands or the curious pointed chin. She was at the edge of some mystery, dizzy as if at the edge of a cliff. She noticed how the hair grew far forward on his temples. She felt the texture of each hair.

They sat in silence now. Elizabeth became aware of the voice of the man at the next table.

"It's a real break," he was saying, "a chance to learn the whole operation, but without too much responsibility at first."

The waitress was standing by the edge of the bar, a couple of the rhinestones on her glasses glittering in the light. Two students sat at a table in the corner of the room leaning forward over glasses of beer to talk. The face of one seemed familiar, but she couldn't place it. He had a beard, but where-ever she had seen him before he'd been clean shaven.

"I'll give it a year," the voice was saying, "then I'll either apply to become a branch manager or get out of it altogether. That's the plan I've got in mind."

Elizabeth couldn't see the window, but when someone opened the door she heard the sound of the rain still pouring down, and the sound of car wheels hissing over the wet pavement. She wanted Robert to speak to her, to draw her toward him.

"Do you feel the energy in yourself?" he said.

"Sometimes it's all inside, and I feel that my head can't hold it."

"That's what your body's for."

"What?"

"To let you out of your mind."

"Or into your mind." Yes, suddenly that was true. "Have you read Saint-Denys Garneau?"

"No."

"He makes me feel the edges of things, the mind and the body and space. He says we don't know how to play with space."

"He's probably right."

"You should read him."

"My French isn't good any more."

"You can get some things in English, the journal and a few of the poems."

Elizabeth saw the waitress coming toward the table. She had pleasant eyes behind the decorative glasses, and Elizabeth found herself smiling pointlessly at her as if by coming to the table she were offering some unexpected gift.

"Do you want anything else?" she said.

"Could I have more coffee?" Elizabeth said, and Robert ordered two more cups.

"I must be happy," Elizabeth said after the woman left. "I

74

was smiling at that waitress as if she were a long-lost friend."

Robert's eyes meeting hers were puzzled.

"You're a curious person," he said.

"Yes I am. In both senses. I'm both a nut and a snoop. All my life I've been terribly curious, wanting to know about things."

"Freud says somewhere that all curiosity is sexual, the little child wanting to know what his parents do after they close their door."

Elizabeth felt a chill somewhere in her bones. Her parent's door *was* magic.

"You should take the time to read Garneau," she said. "Do you like Baudelaire?"

"Very much."

"Then you'd like Garneau. He often talks about Baudelaire in his journal."

"One good Jansenist deserves another."

"You really think that I have a thing about Jansenists."

"You do. But it's understandable. There's something attractive about their intensity. But I'm not sure I'd want my daughter to marry one."

"You're just teasing me."

"I suppose I am."

"I don't mind, really. I get too serious sometimes, and it's good for me to be laughed at. My father used to make me take my mind off myself that way." Again she felt him disappear. "What is it?"

"Nothing."

"I don't really feel that you're older than I am. Age doesn't really change people."

Their eyes met and his did not move away. Now there was this moment.

"Shall we go?" he said.

The film ran backwards, taking them to the door of the restaurant, running back through the rain to the car, through the wet streets side by side to her apartment.

"Why not come in?"

"Sure."

As they walked to the door Elizabeth felt as if she were the air and the rain was falling through her. There was another shape that held them both, and she did not question it; she was blind and deaf and mute. They entered her room and she crossed to close the curtains and turned to him. For now he belonged here. He would hold her. They would kiss as if they knew no other language.

6

Robert paid the blond woman pharmacist for the package of safes. Behind her on a shelf he noticed a large box with a multitude of plastic containers of birth-control pills piled one on top of the other.

On the way out of the store he glanced at the magazine rack where the sex books and magazines were proliferating. Odd that druggists, ignorant men in white jackets, had become the priesthood of sexual pleasure. He looked at the *Playboy* calendars, the copies of *The Story of O* and *Fanny Hill*. He put the package of safes in his pocket and walked out of the store, remembering a sentence from Freud that he had once copied into a notebook.

I think the possibility must be considered that something in the nature of the sexual instinct itself is unfavourable to the achievement of absolute gratification.

Robert walked out to the street. The previous week had been a curious combination of satisfaction and tense restraint. He hadn't made love to Elizabeth, but through the hours of talk, of long complex kisses, she had come to accept the idea as a possibility. Still her fear always triumphed, and once or twice

76

he had lost his temper, felt a surge of anger and desire that made his hands weapons. She would withdraw from him into a strange silence, her eyes glittering in absence, and Robert would hold himself rigid, asking why he went through this instead of finding any one of dozens of more accommodating women. Did he need this, always to be on the edge of pain, given drama and significance by difficulty? Certainly all week he had felt intensely conscious.

It seemed that half his life was spent in her pale room listening to the torrent of her words or lost in her mouth, her hair. To be there was like being somewhere else, in another life, on another planet. At the bottom of the stairs was the Victorian stained-glass window, the young knight, slender, almost effeminate, translucent blue and green and amber. Then stairs and the room, the bed, the single chair. The smell of her hair.

The previous night he had told her that he would buy himself some contraceptives. She had not looked at him, not spoken, but there was a kind of acceptance in her silence, no hostility. They both knew that he would enter her long white body, but neither knew when it would happen.

The air was clear and cool as Robert walked up Princess Street, the light sloping from the sun, which moved west and south. Everything was defined in that light. Strange autumn light like the previous Monday, Thanksgiving Day, when he went out by the lake with Elizabeth, watching while she snapped pictures. He tried to talk to her about the FLQ kidnappings. Politics bored her, even the dramatic actions of fanatics; he tried to explain his odd sense of how the kidnappings created a secret at the heart of Montreal that was truer than the efficient movement of traffic.

Then, as they sat in the park, the light shone at a sharp angle and with a strange colour, almost green, with dark storm clouds moving behind it. The wind blew in powerful gusts. The movement of branches in the strange light and against the backdrop of the moving clouds created in them both an odd breathless excitement. They sat on a bench pointing out to each other the changes of light and leaf-shape and cloud. They saw with the same eyes. Everything in the world was immediate, unpredictable, as if the sudden surprise of the kidnapping was the most likely of events. Anywhere a car might stop and strange men give their messages, make their demands.

Back at Elizabeth's apartment, they ate the dinner she had cooked, a roast chicken, salad, muffins. Robert was surprised that she was a good cook, she didn't seem the type. He had brought wine, and after dinner they sat by the window and Elizabeth took out her photograph album and showed him pictures of her family and friends. She seemed younger doing this, far away from him.

One of the photographs remained vivid in his mind. It was a picture of Elizabeth with her grandfather, her mother's father. He had been a farmer and died within a year or so after the photograph was taken. He was wearing overalls and a straw fedora and staring at the camera. One of his eyelids drooped conspicuously. Elizabeth stood beside him, just the height of his chest, her face framed in dark hair. In the distance was a barn.

The photograph made Robert uneasy when he remembered it now. The solid reality of the farm world, the awkward stance of the man, the strength of his big hands, Elizabeth's place within a family; all these things came together to make him feel alien, unreal. He had never worked with his hands, nor had his father or grandfather. They were city men, images attached to buildings. Robert had little sense of family. Somewhere, perhaps, he might have a photograph of his mother and father, but he had no sense of having grown within the rich branching of a family history. His people left and didn't look back, not out of courage so much as a simple lack of feeling. They didn't care.

Robert resolved again to visit his father. He didn't like his father and his father didn't like him, but he must make the gesture.

As Robert walked up the street, he had been half watching the store windows. He noticed that one of the men's stores was having a sale. He continued up the street for a few feet, then stopped and walked back. His clothes were all getting badly worn, the best of them things he had bought years before. The cardigan he was wearing had a thin spot on the elbow that would soon wear through. He hadn't thought of buying clothes recently; everything in his life had seemed too temporary.

Inside the store, he walked toward the back where there was a display of sweaters, walked past the dark solid colours of the place, conventionally masculine, conventionally tasteful. He felt uncomfortable. The clerk behind the counter, a short bald man with a grey suit and a pink face, was looking at him, considering whether to attack. Robert made himself look slowly through the pile of sweaters. They were good English wool at a reasonable price and they appealed to him. He settled on a dark green cardigan. As he turned to the front of the store with the cardigan in his hand, he saw Ray Statler walk in the door and move to a wooden rack where packages of underwear were displayed. Ray picked up three small packages and turned, seeing Robert for the first time and waving a hand, as they both moved toward the counter.

"I didn't think you ever bought new clothes, Robert," he said.

"Not often, but when they start to get full of holes I have to do something."

The bald clerk waited for them, his eyes cold behind rimless glasses. Ray put his purchases on the counter, expecting to be served first. The boxes contained French bikini underwear. Robert was surprised at the price.

"Expensive," he said, indicating the boxes.

"It's important to let your cock know that you care," Ray said. The old man behind the counter pursed his lips as he wrote the bill. He put the three packages in a bag.

"Why don't we go and have a drink?" Ray said as he took the package from the man's hand. "Good way to celebrate Saturday afternoon."

"Sure."

The clerk checked the price on Robert's sweater and began to write a bill.

"Are you going to Alma's party tonight?"

"I think so." Elizabeth hadn't much wanted to go to the party, but Alma was the university business administrator who dealt with their office and Robert liked her and felt he should put in an appearance.

"Want me to fix you up with a friend of Margita's?"

"I'm doing quite well on my own, Ray."

"Great. Maybe that grey-around-the-eyeballs bachelor look will go away."

Robert picked up his parcel and his change.

"Could be."

They walked out of the store and turned down the street toward the La Salle. Ray Statler walked with his head thrown a little back, whistling between his teeth. They entered the La Salle through a confusion of bodies coming and going through the door, and made their way to a table in the Persian Room. It was dark and almost empty. They gave their order and Ray spread himself out in his chair, legs across the floor.

"What do you think of the latest gesture by our swinging prime minister?" he said.

"He's crazy. The War Measures Act is the most dangerous thing he could have done. The man obviously doesn't even understand parliamentary democracy."

"That's why I like him. He doesn't take any shit from anybody."

"I'll bet you think Hitler was a great political leader."

The waiter came and set down on the table Ray's beer and Robert's gin and tonic. Robert paid for the two drinks.

"Actually I once did a series of prints based on old photographs of Hitler. There's something interesting about him, but he was nuts. Trudeau isn't nuts."

"So much the worse. He could destroy the country."

"He's giving the people what they want. Everybody likes to feel that the government's active and involved. So he did something. Ordinary people love it. Only liberals like you object."

"There was no need for it. The police had all the power they needed."

"The police in Quebec will be going crazy, won't they? Beating everybody in sight."

"You're a cynic."

"I don't know how a man your age can be so naïve. He's got style anyway. 'Go ahead and bleed.' "

"He's going to destroy this country," Robert said. He was becoming terribly angry. Something in him broke loose. "It's old fashioned to believe in democracy and civil liberties. Everybody's too goddam sophisticated for that now. We just open our legs when we're told and make a few cool jokes while we're geting fucked. I'm naïve, I expect too much. I have this foolish belief that the people in a community know what's best for them."

"If there was an election tomorrow, he'd get 90 percent of the votes. Including Quebec."

"That doesn't make it right. Sure people are scared. We don't know how big the FLQ is, but that's not the point. He's flattering people's fears. If a kid has a nightmare, you don't get a shotgun and start blasting all the suspicious shapes in the corners of his room. You talk to him and turn on the lights."

Robert picked up his drink and took a large swallow. He looked across at the handsome face with the rich coloured beard. He wanted to scream.

"You know the price of everything, Ray."

"What's that mean?"

"It's half an aphorism. . . . Never mind. Everybody knows

the price of everything. It's our religion. Have you heard of Nechayev?"

"No."

"Neither have I."

Robert took another drink.

"Take it easy, Robert. I don't believe in politics. That makes you mad, but it's true. I believe in my cock and my talent. And that's all."

"Can you live with that?"

"I seem to be managing." He sipped his beer. "Do you think the FLQ are serious enough to kill Cross and Laporte?"

"No, they're idealists. Sometimes idealists go berserk but I don't think they will. They have too much to lose. The whole point of this kind of gesture is to rouse people, make them notice, ask themselves questions. Maybe to make people believe that it is possible to act, to take control of your own life. Maybe to make us realize that we *don't know* what it feels like to be them."

"It must be crazy in Montreal right now. Half the city in jail."

"It's like some kind of bad melodrama. The evil FLQ planning to destroy us all, Trudeau's army riding out to the rescue. Banners saying *Vive le Québec libre* and National Unity. Everything gives us the feeling that they're huge and hidden and mysterious, like some kind of lethal bacteria. They're not people trying to say something. They're bacteria. So we get a massive dose of antibiotic. It's like a nightmare. Then one morning we wake up and all the laws are changed."

"What would be great is to do some prints of Trudeau with pieces from the newspaper reports. You could use bleeding hearts all over them."

"Why in hell do I try and talk politics to unpolitical people?"

"Let's have another drink."

"Sure, why not? Nothing's going to happen. Nothing ever really happens."

Robert wondered if there was anyone who would understand his feeling. Jennifer perhaps; they had moved in the same political circles in university and there was some hangover of concern in both. He was tempted to phone her; he needed someone to hear what he was saying. He had tried to tell Elizabeth, but when he tried to talk about politics, she stopped listening.

In the drugstore were shelves of sexual treats. All those chemicals, all those fantasies put out so that no-one had to live truly; truth now was two bodies panting in unison. What he himself had been telling Elizabeth. There was some connection hidden from him, something that held these pieces together, some unity of passion that could reassemble the pieces of the broken world. Was that simply absurd, like wanting to find the one woman who would embody all your needs, would make you secure and set you free all at once?

Something in the nature of the sexual instinct itself is unfavourable to the achievement of absolute gratification. Or we would be gods. We take a moment's comfort, a moment's pleasure in the barren fields of the disastrous commonwealth; our neighbours are strangers.

"A political leader should appeal to what's best in us, not what's worst and weakest. He defines the political choices that we make, and if he defines them crudely, we have no hope."

"Drink up, Robert. You're not going to get me to take politics seriously. Find some nice young thing and give her a good unpolitical fuck. You'll feel a lot better."

Robert avoided looking at him. Drank the rich bitter-tasting liquid from his glass.

"Margita would take you seriously. Her family left Czechoslovakia in a hurry, and she's very political; my attitude makes her mad too. You got a nice face when you're excited. If I had a pencil I'd draw you."

Robert couldn't sit with him any longer; his shoulders were hunched against the intensity of anger in his chest and belly.

He stood up.

"Someday," he said, the words coming swiftly, without apparent thought, "you're going to get tired of playing with your cock, and you're going to reach out for something, and it won't be there, and you won't even know what it was you were reaching for. Well, it will be some kind of human dignity you'll be reaching for, and it won't be there because so many people said that politics weren't important."

Robert walked away. He was disgusted with himself for being provoked into that empty litle speech. Preaching to the deaf, and who was he to preach? A private man who lived in a grim apartment and spent his free time trying to seduce a neurotic child.

The bearded prophets fade in my brain from prophet to hero to small personal ghosts. I will walk the streets in the next election. I will write an essay on the need for a rebirth of politics. I will study Aristotle. I will read the newspaper more carefully. Old prophets, don't fade into ghosts. Walk with me along these streets.

Robert walked on with the sensation of being nowhere, living nowhere, being a kind of floating particle. His only connection with the world was his desire for Elizabeth's body.

When he reached his apartment he mixed himself a drink and sat staring at the telephone, wondering if he should phone Jennifer. He reached out, lifted the phone and put it down. Did the same once again and this time dialed the numbers, each one with an effort of will. It rang three times, maybe she was out.

"Hello." Gavin's voice.

"Hi Gavin, it's Dad. Is your mother there?"

"No, she's out somewhere. I just got back from the airport with Mark. We rode our bikes out."

"That's a long way."

"It's not really very far. We saw a couple of planes take off."

"Great."

"Do you want Mum to phone you?"

"No."

There was an awkward silence.

"Well, I'll see you tomorrow, Gavin. Maybe we'll go out in the country."

"Okay Dad. So long."

7

Robert was gone and the faces surrounded her. Eyes were staring at her. A face, wide and flat with pale hair and a thick pale moustache under the short nose. It had the fierce concentration of a small stupid dangerous animal. Rancour was its native element.

"They should be put in front of a firing squad. When the cops get them they should just execute them on the spot. Let all the bleeding hearts in to watch."

He loved the phrase. His dullness came to a focus in the self-importance with which he drew it to himself and caressed it. He was one of those people with a voluptuous appetite for cliché. There was a gleam of conquest in his little eyes.

She looked for Robert and couldn't find him. Some kind of fear was growing in her, and she was finding it hard to breathe. She turned toward the door and met another face; it had a narrow moustache and wet sensitive eyes with a psychotic flicker behind them. The face smiled at her. It had narrow teeth. The sensitive eyes flickered damply at her. The mouth opened and spoke breathily. She tried to smile and turned away; she felt dizzy from the noise and smoke. She could see nothing but eyes and mouths. Earlier she had been introduced to the man Robert worked with, Ray something. He stood nearby now, laughing loudly and watching her out of the corner of his eyes. She turned away.

Lips pursed around a joint of grass sucked deliciously backward. Nearby, sensitive eyes followed her. From behind an oily effeminate voice greeted her.

"Hello there, good to see you." The mouth simpered. Each greasy hair held its place. She nodded and made her way toward the door.

She wondered what was wrong with her. It wasn't a bad party. She had been at worse; no-one here had thrown up on the floor or started to fight, but she had to get out. The faces all seemed like huge lumps of flesh driven by a demonic power. She found herself studying ears and nostrils. She knew many of these people, by appearance if not by name. Eyes. Mouths that reached hungrily out toward hers, fed on her until she choked and ran in panic. Where was Robert? He must be in another room. She didn't know whether to go out and get some air or try and find him; for a moment she felt the panicky fear that he had gone with some easier woman and left her. She turned toward the door. Met sensitive eyes. Ravenous eyes. They fed on her like giant insects.

She caught a glimpse of Robert in the next room and waited for a group to move past her and let her make her way toward him. He was talking to a rather short, heavy-bodied woman with dark braided hair pinned up on her head. As she watched their faces for a few seconds, Elizabeth realized that this must be his wife. There was a curious quickness in the way they responded to each other.

Elizabeth stood, paralyzed. She could move neither toward nor away, but stared at the two of them, fascinated by the way their eyes flickered, not daring to meet. It was as if they stood in some kind of enchanted circle of shared experience and were too uneasy to notice it. Elizabeth looked at Robert's face.

To her left, she saw a door open. Someone came out of the bathroom. Quickly Elizabeth walked in and locked the door behind her. The window was open, and she could feel a cool breeze from it; she walked to it and put her mouth against the narrow opening, breathing in the cold air greedily. She sat down on the toilet and the dizziness eased a little. She put her hands over her eyes and rocked back and forth, hidden in the darkness of her mind.

She didn't want to see Robert's wife as a person; she couldn't deal with persons, had no words to encounter the incomprehensible possibilities of faces, voices, hearts. There ought to be a formula of words. Elizabeth thought of the woman as she had seen her standing by Robert, her mind attempting again to recognize her as Robert's wife, the woman who had held him inside her body, created his children. She was so much shorter than Robert that they looked odd together; he and Elizabeth were a better match. She thought of the woman's large breasts and wondered if Robert missed their softness. Suddenly Elizabeth knew she must meet her.

As she went back out into the room, they were still talking, although it looked as if Robert was about to turn away. Elizabeth walked directly to them and smiled at Robert.

"Elizabeth," he said, "this is Jennifer."

Elizabeth put out her hand. She wanted to touch the woman. The skin of Jennifer's hand was warm.

"I'm glad to meet you," Jennifer said.

Elizabeth smiled. The woman seemed to mean what she said.

"You're a very beautiful girl," she went on.

Elizabeth could not speak, found the woman's dark eyes holding her. She didn't know what was happening and could find no words with which to meet the dark eyes that were looking through her. Jennifer reminded her a little of Martha and that made her seem familiar, took away the defence of distance.

"You look a little like an old friend of mine," Elizabeth said.

"Someone in Kingston?"

"No. She's in England now. We write each other all the

time. I suppose she's my most important friend."

Elizabeth sensed that she was babbling and stopped herself. The three of them stood in silence. Jennifer was like Martha, self-contained, able to stand in silence, looking perfectly easy with it. Her calm expressive face with the beginnings of wrinkles around the eyes and mouth, the full small body, all made Elizabeth feel young and important. Why had she been so terrified of the strange faces, of the hostility? This woman had no fear of it.

"I'm going to go and get another drink," Jennifer said. "It's nice to have met you, Elizabeth."

She walked away. Elizabeth turned and found Robert's eyes were hidden.

"She's neat," Elizabeth said.

"Is she?"

"She seems very solid."

"It's a pretty good performance, but then I've seen it more often than you."

"She could have been nasty to me."

"No. That would have put her in the wrong and allowed me to be angry and comfort you. She behaved beautifully Makes it clear to me and you both that whatever happened between us must be my fault."

"I liked her."

"I noticed."

"You're angry."

"Frustrated. Let's have another drink."

"Can we go soon?"

"I'd like to have another drink first. I don't like to feel tha Jennifer's driven me out."

"Okay, but don't leave me alone. I don't like it. I don't lik having to meet people or look at them."

He reached out and squeezed her hand. He led her towar the kitchen, where the drinks were. They passed through dark room filled with noise and the strong smoke of dope.

was a smell foreign to her nose. Beside the kitchen door a girl leaned against the wall, her hands in the front pockets of her blue-jeans, her face wary, almost sullen. Elizabeth's eyes met hers for a second and they both looked away, unwilling to explore the possibilities of meeting.

The light was turned on in the kitchen, and the faces all seemed to have a different quality, more self-conscious. In the corner of the room Elizabeth saw another of her former professors, who smiled at her and turned back to the nervous-looking woman beside him. It was clear from the way he talked that it was not his wife, but it looked like the sort of woman he would be married to.

Robert mixed himself a strong gin and tonic and got Elizabeth a glass of ginger ale. She had been drinking wine at dinner and vermouth for the first part of the evening, and she knew if she drank more she would start to feel strange and lost again. If Robert stayed with her she would be all right; so long as he was closer to her than anyone else they could not harm her.

She looked at the glass of ginger ale in her hands, surprised that she had hands, as always when she came back out of her mind, the grey geography of those inner events, startled to have hands, feet. To be her was to be this. She looked down at the white dress where it went round the wide pelvis. To be her was to be this. Robert was a feeling inside her, now of comfort, at times of fear. Robert was this tall man with a long face, all the lines in it drawing downward, almost clownish. Robert was a man who had penetrated the bodies of women, of that small dark woman who had spoken kindly to her. She looked across the room at the body of the thin nervous woman, of the girl in jeans just beyond the door. Bodies of women. To be her was to be this. She remembered Jennifer calling her beautiful. Was it really to hinder Robert? Did she somehow take any of her beauty out of his eyes by speaking of it?

They walked back out of the kitchen, past the silent girl

who watched them pass. They found a space next to a set of bookshelves and Robert leaned against the wall.

"You okay?" he said.

"All right now. For a while I couldn't find you, and I get panicky when I'm alone in a crowd. I start to feel I'm drowning."

"But you're the one who wins the swimming races."

"I forgot I'd told you that."

She saw Robert's eyes move toward two men who were standing near them arguing.

"Bourassa was crumbling," one of them said. "There was nothing else to do. You've got to control the streets. You don't need all that much to start students rioting, look at France, look at Latin America. And if you lose control of the streets, then the ordinary respectable people get frightened. After that anything can happen. A *coup d'état*. Anything. You've got to give people reassurance first and then go after the specific political problems."

She could see the tension in Robert's face. It made her feel helpless to know how disturbed he was and not to be able to respond. She could only imagine the fear felt by the kidnapped men, that plain emotion was clear to her, but social and political ideas meant nothing to her. They were like gibberish. Even Martha, sometimes, would start to talk in a way that made no sense to her; she respected Martha's ideas, she respected Robert's, but she couldn't imagine the motives of the kidnappers or of the government. She thought of men tied up in small rooms, imagined herself tied, men with guns and knives.

The voices went on. She half recognized the names; Bourassa, Ryan, Lévesque. Quebec frightened her, was that a political feeling? She had been to Montreal. Her father took her to Montreal, she remembered the pain. She heard Robert's voice.

"Political civilization is based on trust," he said. "Destroy that trust, and there's no way back to it. The law isn't worth anything if it has to be enforced. For a country to survive, it has to learn to pit trust and reason against violence. It doesn't have the appeal of melodrama. There's no magic to it. But it's necessary."

One of the men turned to Robert. He had thin features and steel-rimmed glasses and a neat beard.

"You sound like a philosophical anarchist," he said. "Anarchists have wonderful ideas, but they always lose. They make noble martyrs."

Robert just nodded. One of his phrases began to go round in Elizabeth's head. There's no magic to it. He'd said that to her, his hand stroking her breasts; it's not magic, he'd said, it's just pleasure. No magic; her body was not a door sealed by a curse, did not need the incantation, only his gradual patient speaking and waiting. It was simple, he said, it was only pleasure. Something Martha had said in a letter that she remembered: women are all magic, they have no bodies, only emanations from their spiritual selves and men hate this mystery and want them to be only bodies. All men hate magic.

Now again Robert said, There is no magic, denying it. But perhaps politics was magic for men who spoke that language.

She looked toward Robert, could see that his face was knotted with tension, with anger, feared that he would turn the anger on her. Because she could not understand. She felt suddenly free and loving. To be her was to be this. Holding him against her breasts instead of his wife's; she willed him to look toward her and he did, and she felt breathless with freedom. He held her eyes and didn't look away. His head made a motion toward the door, and she nodded.

They got their coats and left, the cold clear air shocking them awake. Robert put his arm around her, and they moved silently along the street toward his apartment. She had never been there before, but now she wanted to go there, to go anywhere he was going. He was part of the magic. She contained him.

The house that held his apartment was rather ordinary, and the apartment itself seemed bare, half empty, the locus of a dim solitude that she wanted to enter, to dispel. She would find the incantation for it. She was rich and daring.

He had turned on the lights and taken her coat, and now they stood like sculptures in the bald light of the living-room. Elizabeth could not speak, but reached toward him with her eyes, holding him, and he came and led her to the bedroom, turning off the overhead light so that the apartment was in darkness except for a bit of light coming through the curtains from a streetlight outside. Elizabeth did not know where she was; she was in an anonymous darkness telling a story and being in the story she was telling, describing her actions as she unfastened her dress, took off each article of clothing. This did not happen, she did not do this.

Robert's hands moved, discovering, he drew her toward the bed. It was warm, strangely comfortable to be there with him, and she felt young, remembered the warmth of sharing Tom's bed, how he would be pleased with her. She liked to be held like this, but now when she kissed him it was different; before, the kisses had seemed timeless, their mouths were lost in themselves, but now she could feel in his mouth that he was urging her somewhere, taking her over boundaries. His hands caressed her, his mouth caressed her and she felt herself begin to desire him. What was the thing that moved in her? Magic? Pleasure? A girl was lying in the arms of this man and her breathing was changing. His penis was erect and seemed too big. She had forgotten. She wanted it to be over, to be herself again.

He moved away from her, and she was shocked, frightened. There were noises as he put on the safe, and he came back to her, but he would not just do it and let her go. He held her and stroked her; she pushed him away, said no, but he talked to her and was suddenly not a stranger, was Robert and she held him. She would hold him as softly as anyone could.

Thought of his wife's rich body and felt thin and poor, but held him and kissed his mouth.

He moved over her. She was young and small and he would hurt her. She pulled away, and again he talked, gentled her. She felt the panic of a wild bird held in the hand, but as it flowed away, he was inside her moving. Her breath was not her own, and strange bright feelings spread out from her spine into all her bones. She pushed urgently for it to be over, but it wasn't and her breath came back to match his. She lost him. He was unknown. He was not a man, only this instrument that opened her. She did not want to want it. He moved. It moved. Her heart beat fast like a trapped bird's heart. This was too soft and terrible and something lifted him, she tried to reach him, running, flying. He cried out, he was wounded too. He fell.

She wanted to hold and comfort him, but her arms were stiff, lost. He murmured and she felt tears come for him, he was so sweet and naked, but she was no help to him. She would always fail him. He was quiet now and lay softly on her. She wanted to hold him but her body was still alight and tensed and far away. He moved and drew away from her and spoke and then she felt wounded all over her body, her spirit pouring through her skin like blood, as if she would die. She looked at the line of light across the ceiling following it over to the wall and down. She closed her eyes and vanished from him, from herself. Who was she now? It had not been like this with Tom, she was always contained, safe. He found comfort, there was not this danger.

Robert shifted position. His hand found her breast and held it.

"I'm half asleep," he said. "Are you?"

"No."

"Do you want to get up and we'll have some tea or coffee?"

She could hear the sleep creeping into his voice.

"You go to sleep," she said.

"Good night." He shifted position, and within a couple of minutes she could tell he was asleep. She felt strange to be in the bed with him, strained her eyes to see the room then didn't want to know the unfamiliar shapes. It was only pleasure; do it and sleep. If so, she was unchanged, untouched by it, and in a way she felt that, hard and distant and immovable, listening to the sounds of his sleep.

She got quietly out of bed and searched in the dark for her clothes. It was hard to find them and sort them out and she spent nearly a minute on her hands and knees searching for a lost shoe. For a few desperate seconds she thought of walking home in her stockings carrying one shoe, but she soon after laid her fingers on the other.

There was a streetlight just outside the living-room window of the apartment so she had no difficulty in finding her coat. She let herself out quietly and walked down the stairs.

When she reached the street, there was a moment of disorientation. It was so simple and familiar that she didn't know how to respond. It was gone, had never happened. Where was she? In a second she had found all the events, seen them from the outside and assured herself of their reality. Then turned to walk home.

The streets were empty, and she met no-one. As if the world had been abandoned. Or as if she could see no-one because she was invisible. She walked. The streets were empty.

When she reached her room, she undressed and got into bed without turning on the light; she wanted to remain invisible now, was afraid to see her face. She lay in bed on her back, very still, hardly breathing. Waited for sleep.

She woke in sunlight. In her dream she had been travelling through a large building by canoe. Members of her family and people from her university classes were in many rooms having parties and banquets. She was paddling the canoe with great skill under a set of chandeliers that seemed about to fall. At that moment suddenly she was awake and the sunlight was bright on the rug beside her. She had forgotten to close the curtains. Why?

In sleep anything could be forgotten. Now she remembered the previous night. Not to think of it yet, she pushed herself from the bed and into the bathroom, got in the shower and soaped herself energetically.

His wife had said that Elizabeth was beautiful; Robert had entered, inhabited her body; she had wanted him, had felt what she could remember but not credit. The soap seemed to burn her skin as she washed. Moved away from the dream.

She dressed. The clothes covered her skin, created her. Made the bed. Prepared to make coffee, but decided that she didn't want to be still and took out her jacket and set out to walk by the lake. Following the familiar street, toward the blessing of the water.

The air was brilliantly clear, and as Elizabeth came to the edge of the water, she could see every detail of the island, the trees, the brown earth, a barn that seemed to shine with an almost supernatural clarity. Every detail pressed into her eyes. Robert seemed still inside her, invading her with a terrible slow insistence. She walked faster and felt her skin glisten against the shining air. She began to run. Saw herself running, hair in the wind. Robert pursuing her, and as she ran faster to escape, she only brought him closer until the rhythm of her running seemed to be the rhythm of his movement inside her. She stopped running and stood still, holding herself tight against the iron railing, the skin of her face tight and shining, terrified, the water and sky brilliant blue, a soft lap of waves on the pebbles at her feet. She could not get rid of Robert's presence inside her, the slow, dim blunt moving of him. He was fucking her. It was like a wound. It seemed as if she would never be free of it, the stranger who lay on her and invaded her. Because she wished it. Her own desire seemed to her like some grotesque appendage to herself, some strange thing she had grown in the night. A cancer, a lump. She saw a small

95

thin figure at the edge of bright water carrying a great dark burden.

A child burdened with desire. But she wasn't a child. She was a woman and had conceived. She felt a chill on her back at the thought that the safes wouldn't work, that Robert would make her pregnant.

A teenage boy with long blond hair was walking along the cement path toward her with a young German Shepherd. The dog galloped toward her to look and sniff. At first Elizabeth kept her face turned away, not wanting the boy to see it, but suddenly she turned and patted the dog.

"What's your dog's name?" she said. Strange, that she could talk. The boy was wearing tight jeans and she could see the bulge of his genitals. She was surprised at herself noticing and stood upright.

"His name's Bismarck. He's a purebred but I don't have his papers."

"It's a nice day, isn't it?" Elizabeth said. Deliberately. To end the conversation. The boy nodded and walked away, snapping his fingers for the dog to follow him, then beginning to run, the dog moving beside him and making leaps toward his moving arms. Elizabeth turned away from the water and walked toward her room. In the clear air, the figures that moved down side streets or across the green shaded lawn of the park seemed precise and mechanical. It was like being in an airplane and looking down on the miniature city below.

The windows of the old houses watched her as she made her way back to the stillness of her room. The grey stone courthouse maintained a judicial calm.

Her room was still, calm, white and blue and pale blue. She made herself a cup of coffee and sat in the window. In safety. He could not reach her here. She took the phone off the hook, and holding the coffee in her hands, letting the warmth move into her fingers, she relaxed into stillness. Her body returned to her. Time flowed smooth as water. An old woman, a favourite of Elizabeth's, passed by below, bent and toothless, carrying a plastic shopping-bag, her feet appearing to move quickly though her actual progress along the street was very slow. Elizabeth smiled as she watched her. She had many window-friends, people she knew from watching them pass by. Robert wanted to destroy this blue stillness but she wouldn't allow it. He was gone from inside her now. She was safe.

She moved through the room.

She undressed and put on a long dressing-gown and moved through the room like an elegant ghost, her gown whispering as it brushed the floor. She turned on the radio to look for music. The first station she turned to was playing something serious, almost mournful.

By now the sun had risen to the point where it began to shine in the windows of her room. Elizabeth sat on the floor in a patch of sunlight on the small fluffy white rug, her hands clasped around her knees, almost listening to the music.

Head down, eyes open, soft and happy as a cat in sunlight. She moved her toes slowly, watched the articulation of the joints as they moved in and out of a small patch of shadow.

Words. News.

The dead body of Pierre Laporte had been found in the trunk of a car in the suburbs of Montreal. The dead body. The body. A dead body curled dead in the trunk of a late-model car. The car and the body, curled. The dead body in the back of the car curled, bleeding wounded inside, screaming inside, the dead body curled in the back of the mind.

We'll just forget about it, Lizzie. It never happened. Everyone has the right to one mistake, and now we're going to forget about this. The pills he gave you will take the pain away soon. You'll fall asleep soon and we'll be home, and in a couple of days we'll have forgotten all about it.

The body curled around its wound. Curled like a secret child, like Elizabeth curled on the floor in sunlight on a white rug. In a suburb of Montreal. A doctor with a strange accent and eyes that looked friendly although he didn't say one friendly word, as she left said *Try not to come back* and the nurse smiled.

She hadn't imagined. Couldn't imagine the pain. All she knew was that she must hold it inside herself, hold her pain like a rich gift, that if she screamed the world could come apart in the pieces of her scream.

Her father wrapped her in a blanket in the back of his car and drove and talked to her (and the shadow of his death, soon, soon, rode beside him in the seat) and now Elizabeth knew that the shadow had been there and thought perhaps she had even known it then.

Whatever you've done, Lizzie, you've more than paid for, so just forget and we'll try to forget. Philip doesn't know anything about it and we're not going to tell him. It's over with now. Tom's going to England for six months. His father and I decided that was the best thing. When you go back to school it will all be over.

The wheels singing on the road, Elizabeth curled tight, her eyes shut, hoarding her pain like gold. Her father's voice went on, binding her tighter. She was always somehow in danger. They invaded her body with instruments, the doctor with his shining steel spoon, Robert with his blunt slow thing, and she had to go into hiding again, down somewhere to safety.

She sat up and went to the radio. Turned it off. Went and lay down on the bed, lying on her back, straight and still. He fucked her, dim and insistent. She must get rid of him somehow. Decided to phone and tell him she wouldn't see him again. Then phone Burtch and ask him to take her to a movie. Yes. Yes.

8

The weather was clear and cool. So would be his internal weather now. He would put his life in order. The body and soul of that shining girl; the way was not clear, but there was a way. His desire had a pattern that was defined and mysterious. He was beginning again. He no longer wanted comfort; he wanted a brilliant difficult fate.

It was odd how she had vanished after Saturday night. He had wakened yesterday morning and found her gone. When he phoned her apartment during the morning there was no answer, and in the afternoon he had taken Gavin and Cindy out in the country for a long walk through the woods. It was a bright day, marvellous for walking, and the woods were brilliant and beautiful. They went on for miles until they came to a lake, then sat on the shore among the fallen leaves until it grew cold. When they got back to the city it was dark, and Robert drove past Elizabeth's apartment. There was no light in the window, and when he phoned there was no answer. It was as if she had disappeared from the earth or never existed, as if, when he left her quiet room, she became immobile, invisible until he returned. She was nothing, the shining mirror of nothing. He remembered the curious, almost anguished excitement of her body under his.

This morning when he got up he had almost phoned her, but had decided instead that he would walk to her apartment at lunch time, perhaps take the afternoon off and spend it with her.

Since last night, when he had heard of the death of Laporte, an idea had been growing in him, an idea that was partly the expression of his own sense that something extraordinary was happening. It was what he had felt in that moment in the park when likelihood seemed to fall away like old clothes. Likelihood might reassert itself, but there was the chance to catch this moment in a book.

The Unexpected Fall. Or *The Unlikely Fall.* Either title. What he must do was find the right material to reflect his sense of being a helpless observer while the universe took a new turn. To know the world was changing but be unable to do more than watch. Four essays, one of his own, very personal to suggest the kind of spiritual weather of the time, one from Ottawa, one from Montreal and one from someplace distant, Vancouver perhaps. Edited so that, almost by indirection, the dangerous drama of the time became clear.

He stood up and walked from his office to the door of Wilson's. Wilson's secretary gave him a fishy glance; she didn't like or trust him and thought that his discussions with Wilson interrupted more important work. Wilson answered his knock, and Robert entered the office. The morning sun caught the corner of the desk and reflected brightly off the brass container of pens and pencils. The painting of the black horse shone slightly in the reflected light.

"I'll get us some coffee," Wilson said. He walked out of the office and spoke to the secretary. Came back and sat down in an armchair beside his desk.

"You're looking well, Robert," he said.

"I feel good, Wilson. I took my children out for a long walk in the country yesterday."

"I'm told exercise is very valuable." There was a gleam of irony in his eye as he said it. Wilson was a happily sedentary man. He walked slowly the few blocks from his house to the office in good weather, but most often his wife drove him.

"I have an idea for a book, Wilson."

"Splendid. Will you tell me about it?"

Robert began to explain the book, and as he talked, Peter Rowsome came into his mind. Peter had been one of his close friends in university. Robert and Peter and Jennifer had shared an interest in what then seemed radical politics and overlapped with an interest in literature. They moved in the circles that dominated student publications. Peter would arrive at Robert's house every now and then with a new political enthusiasm or a new poëm, his round face shining. Peter had gone on to become a lawyer and in 1968 had been elected a Liberal member of parliament for a suburban Toronto constituency. He and Robert had met occasionally when they were both in Toronto, but it had been several months now since they had spoken.

"Who would do the essays?" Wilson asked after Robert finished his sketch of the book's contents.

"I just thought of an old friend of mine who's in Parliament," Robert said. "Peter Rowsome. He's intelligent and literate. And in a way a Liberal backbencher is in the perfect position, in it, but not really in it. He's supposed to be near the centre of power, but I'd like to bet that he's just an observer too. The whole thing is being played out by a few men who somehow embody, or only say they embody, an idea or a set of values."

"That's a very interesting train of thought."

"I suppose I read so much Tolstoy and Marx and Hegel when I was young that the idea of history was very firmly planted in the back of my mind, so I find myself looking at all these dramatic stories in the newspaper and saying 'Here it is.' But then I'm not sure it is. Maybe Canada is a country where history can't happen. Like in 1837."

Robert found ideas coming quickly into his mind, making it hard for him to sit still.

"You must keep me in touch with the project," Wilson said. His secretary knocked on the door and brought in two cups of coffee.

"Very good of you, Evelyn," he said, rising to take the cup from her hand. The old woman smiled in a way that made Robert grimace. She adored Wilson, who flattered her with his best old-world manners.

Robert took his coffee with what he hoped was a pleasant smile. Evelyn Baird looked disapproving and retired, closing the door carefully behind her. He and Wilson sat in silence with their cups of coffee. The brilliant sunlight seemed to make the room expand. Robert wanted to go and tell Elizabeth about the book.

"I think I'll go to Ottawa next week and see Peter. If I can arrange for that piece then I can start to work on the others. I know a few people in Montreal, but not really exactly the ones I want."

"Do you want someone French or English writing from Montreal?"

"French I think."

"I suppose that would raise the problem of whether or not to translate it. One of the many problems of a country that is bilingual in theory but not in practice. I suppose we'd all be better off if we spoke French but it doesn't seem likely to happen."

"It won't happen until it costs money to speak only English."

"More and more we all speak American, don't we, Robert? The subject of many of my unwritten letters to a variety of periodicals. Oh well, there are worse things than to be out of date."

Robert tried but found it hard to imagine Wilson as a young man. He seemed to belong to a class and generation for whom youth was a kind of temporary misfortune to be escaped as quickly as possible. Robert finished his coffee and stood up.

"I think I'll phone Ottawa and try to arrange to see Peter Rowsome next week."

"Yes. That would be a good place to start. Well, do keep me informed."

Robert left the office, went into the small kitchen and washed his coffee cup. He was always careful to do this as a kind of gesture of polite hostility toward Miss Baird. There were two dirty cups left there, probably Ray Statler's, so Robert washed those as well. He felt that put him several points ahead on the day's battle with Miss B.

He went back to his office and phoned Ottawa information, looking for Peter Rowsome's office number. On his first call, he was told that Peter would be back within half an hour, so he filled the time with pointless filing of papers and phoned again. After a bit of secretarial by-play, he heard Peter's voice.

"Robert Mallen, Peter."

"Good to hear from you. It's been too long."

"Yes it has."

"How is everything?"

"Fine. Really very good. Could I come to Ottawa and talk to you next week?"

"What about?"

"I'd like to talk you into doing some writing."

"I gave all that up years ago. You know that."

"Just let me come and talk to you about it. I want to do a book about the kidnappings, but from a number of points of view."

"I'm not sure I'm the man you want."

"Yes you are, but let me come and convince you."

"All right. What about a week from today?"

"Fine. It'll take a couple of hours or so to drive up. Is eleven all right?"

"Yes, that's fine. I'll look forward to seeing you."

The excitement was coming back, the excitement of actually believing in your work, of being committed to it, the thought of creation. He would take Elizabeth to Ottawa with him.

Robert looked over the work on his desk and decided to go to Elizabeth's apartment soon and tell her about the trip to Ottawa. There was nothing very urgent in front of him. As he sat there he heard the front door of the house open and Ray Statler's whistle come toward his office. Ray waved and walked in.

"I did some sketches for that critical book," he said. "I thought we might use one of those prints with a positive super-imposed on a negative but with a different registration."

"Sounds good."

"Yeah, it should work. Might get a sort of ghostly effect. Do it in a bright colour and somebody might actually buy the thing."

"Maybe."

"The next book that comes through we're going to send to Computex for setting. I've had enough of those lousy linotypes."

"You're full of new things today."

"Yeah I am. I feel good. That was a pretty girl you had at the party."

Robert nodded.

"Margita tells me that women would find you very attractive. She says you look sensitive."

"That's what my wife always said. But she also said that looks were deceiving."

"I met your wife at the party. *She* looks sexy."

Was she? Somehow Robert felt that he didn't know. Had he ever known the truth of her? He could remember things about her body, her voice, her responses, but they didn't seem true or inevitable. She might be someone else altogether. With another man, he felt, she would become another person and the woman with whom he'd shared all those years would not exist. His jealousy was partly grief for the loss of that woman.

"I'll show you those sketches in a day or so," Ray said, as he walked out of the office. As soon as he had left, Robert got up and went out.

He got in the car and drove the four or five blocks to Elizabeth's apartment. As he parked the car, he looked up to see if she was sitting in the window, but there was no sign of her. He wondered where she had been all day Sunday and felt a moment's worry about her.

As he walked into the house, the sunlight was shining brightly through the stained-glass window, lighting up the knight in his amber landscape and especially the red centres of the decorative corners. They glowed like rubies. Robert went up the stairs two at a time, tense at the thought that Elizabeth might not be here. As he reached the door, he heard voices inside, one of them a man's voice. He heard Elizabeth laugh. He felt chilled, and nearly turned back down the stairs, but instead, by an effort of will, he raised his hand and knocked.

Elizabeth opened the door. She was wearing a floor-length dressing-gown in a green paisley material. Her hair was tied back in a green ribbon. Behind her Robert could see a man sitting on the bed. He was heavyset and wore a dark suit. His face was vaguely familiar to Robert. There was a record playing softly. Leonard Cohen.

I am a stranger here. I must return to my work and let these children return to theirs.

"Hi," Elizabeth said. "Come on in." Her voice had an intimate quality that had always drawn him, but now it seemed to him merely a mannerism or an accident. He walked into the room. The man on the bed looked toward him and away. Elizabeth introduced them. The young man's name was Wayne Burtch and they shook hands. Then there was silence.

"Do you want some coffee?" Elizabeth said after an empty moment.

"I don't think so," Robert said. "It's nearly lunch time."

That had nothing to do with the coffee, more that he wanted to suggest to Elizabeth that he had come to take her to lunch. The record ended and clicked off.

"Burtch just came and asked me to have lunch with him," she said. Her eyes were on Robert, looking for something. He didn't know what.

"Do you work near here?" Robert said to the man. He knew now why the face was familiar. He had seen him somewhere in Elizabeth's photograph album. He wondered how long she had known him.

"I'm articling with a lawyer down on Brock Street. Craig Wardell."

"The alderman."

"Yeah."

There was another sullen pause in the conversation. Both men sat and waited for Elizabeth to acknowledge one of them or dismiss one of them.

"I tried to phone you yesterday," Robert said to her, "but you seemed to have disappeared."

"I spent a long time out walking and riding my bike. Then I went to a movie."

"I don't understand those English comedies," the young man said.

"They're an acquired taste," Robert said. "It helps to have lived in England." He was stiff and angry. He felt betrayed.

"In a way," Elizabeth said, "they remind me of the old silent comedies. The whole thing is completely unrealistic, but if you accept it, they start to be funny. It's like that for us anyway. Maybe in England they think life's really like that. Maybe it is. I'm always shocked to find that life's like anything. All my ideas came from reading novels, and when the world didn't fit into the shape of the novels, I stopped believing in the world." There was something mannered, self-conscious, about her voice.

Robert wanted to respond, but wouldn't. Let her lawyer give an opinion. Yet after a second's pause he found himself speaking.

"Nothing exists until it's imagined," he said. "As Oscar Wilde said about sunsets."

"Oscar Wilde said everything," Wayne Burtch said. He made it sound as if he had a personal grudge against Wilde.

"I'm sure he tried to," Elizabeth said.

To Robert's surprise, the young man stood up from the bed. The movement seemed to start from his heavy shoulders, the rest of his body following like a tail following a dog.

"I think I'll go, Lizzie," he said. "I'll grab a sandwich and take it back to the office."

"Okay Burtch, thanks for coming round." She went to the door with him and closed it behind him. Robert stood up and walked to her as she turned around. He took her in his arms and kissed her. She kissed him but wasn't there.

"Why did you hide from me yesterday?" he said. Her eyes were close to him, bright and searching.

"I wanted to. I was afraid."

"Of what?"

"You. Me. Saturday night. I don't want to be that vulnerable."

"Why?"

"I just don't. I get all cold and panicky."

"Does running away help?"

"Yes."

"And your lawyer friend?"

"Yes."

"Why?"

"Because most of the time he is just my friend. He doesn't threaten me."

"He was jealous of me."

"Sometimes he thinks he's in love with me, but he isn't really. It's just something for him to think about."

"I hope you don't talk that way about me."

"I don't talk about you at all. Except all the time inside my head and sometimes in my diary. You're my secret."

"I like that." He kissed her again, and this time she was there. He led her to the bed and they lay down there. They lay there together and then she drew her head away.

"Did I ever tell you," she said, "about the time I decided to kill myself?"

"You said you were fascinated by drowning."

"That was how I finally decided to do it. I spent a couple of weeks thinking about it and planning it. I didn't really know why except that death seemed the only real thing. Every day 'd spend hours thinking about how to do it and writing notes in my head that I'd leave. Finally when I decided to do it I didn't leave a note at all. I just walked down to the lake one night and started wading out. When the water was up to my waist, it was cold and I stopped and I could see the moon showing through the clouds and silvering the edges. I heard somebody shout somewhere farther along the shore. Everything was very still, and it was real after all. In fact that was the most real moment I ever remember. So I turned around and came home, soaking wet."

Robert held her in his arms. He had a curious sense that the story was not true, that it was something she had imagined. Sometimes he lost her like this. She became invisible. He held her tighter and kissed her face.

"I'm driving to Ottawa next week," he said. "Do you want to come with me?"

"Sure."

They kissed. She would move slowly toward him like a tide and then draw back in a cold shivering panic. She could give him no sense of what she feared, but he held her and kissed her and stroked her. At last they lay naked side by side, his hands moving over her skin, her body so young and slender and white that it almost hurt him to see it. He found that he was shivering.

He had never known a woman whose pleasure was so dangerous. It created a kind of terrified excitement in him that made him watch her face and then hide from it. The intensity of her awareness almost succeeded in turning this pleasure into magic, pleasure that was like a dream of pain. It was unearthly.

9

They drove north on Highway 15 toward Ottawa, and at the

side of the road were fields where the grass was pale and dead or the ploughed earth dark brown, and, at the edges of the fields, trees or small woodlots, leaves like tongues of fire where the sky touched the earth. The fields seemed to be waiting for something. It was the sense of expectancy that made the fall so exhilarating; the stillness evoked a hundred stories.

They drove through a small town, and each street seemed to lead away into some other reality, as if the past and future were in the air like smoke or a familiar smell. In the yard of a house a small girl played, and the slanting light of the sun that now rose far to the south seemed to make her too real, inapprehensible.

Robert drove in silence. They passed a tree of wild apples that shone a sombre red as the sunlight passed across them. Behind in a field was the rusty wreck of an old panel-truck with the words J. STONE, DELIVERY written on it.

The sky was wide and blue, but in the west a surface of grey clouds was beginning to appear on the horizon. Robert thought of the poems he'd learned in public school about the autumn. They were all obvious, like all the calendars with pictures of brightly coloured maples beside a lake or river, but they were unavoidable. In this strange northern country, fall was the pentecostal season, when the tongues of fire flashed between earth and sky.

He drove on toward Ottawa and the friend of his youth. Peter Rowsome had lived within half a mile of Robert's home in Toronto, but they had not met until university. Robert had often gone to visit Peter's home after that; it had always seemed warmer and more hospitable than his own. There was some tension between Peter and his father, for the father had been an athlete and a great hunter and fisherman, and Peter was interested mainly in ideas and books, but the two of them both joked about it as a source of past conflict. Peter's mother was a kind and possessive woman who had borne only the one child, and even when Robert and Peter were in their twenties, she expected to feed them hugely and protectively, as if they were still young boys.

Although the two of them and Jennifer and some of their friends had talked a lot about politics, they had never belonged to any of the campus political clubs. The LPP communists never seemed very bright and most of the CCF socialists were too infected with Fabian optimism. Now and then, if asked his position, Robert would call himself a Trotskyite, but he used the term very vaguely. Peter had probably never called himself anything, so it wasn't surprising that he had ended in the Liberal party. Still, Robert couldn't help feeling a certain bitter amusement at Peter's position as a backbench Liberal, though his conversion was probably no more surprising than Trudeau's.

When they got close to Ottawa, after a long silence, Elizabeth called his attention to a log house near the road, with two or three log barns beside it. There was a slight curve to the land, and the dry grass was all swept eastward by the wind. The sun glinted on the tin roof.

Robert and Elizabeth had talked little on the trip. Robert found himself wondering what she was thinking, but for now was unwilling to ask. She was still a little mysterious to him. There were tensions that came and went without explanation, but it was less damaging than it had been with Jennifer. The silences left no scars. With Elizabeth it was all a mystery. There seemed to be no issues, no sense of what this all meant. It was a time out of time, an event, like a strange freak of the weather.

Robert glanced across the car. Elizabeth's face was bright, beautiful.

Elizabeth was in the car with me. I can feel her presence all through me. There is no explanation for this. It happened to happen.

Closer to Ottawa, the traffic became heavier. On the Queensway he knew he was in a city, for the cars moved like projectiles. In downtown Ottawa, they stopped and started and crawled toward the Parliament Buildings. He parked in a lot a few blocks away. An army jeep passed by as he was moving into a parking space, and the kidnappings, the political acts were suddenly brought close to him.

"What are you going to do while I talk to Peter?" he said as they climbed out of the car.

"Probably I'll just sit and watch people go by on the Mall. How long will you be?"

"Not too long. Peter was always efficient."

They arranged to meet. Robert leaned over and kissed her before he walked away, and she looked surprised, as if she had been kissed by a complete stranger.

Robert walked up the hill, looking across the grass to where a troop carrier was stationed on one of the driveways leading up to Parliament. He always felt a sense of weight, of mysterious presence when he approached the Parliament Buildings. The human ordinariness, the dirty jokes among the speechwriters in the Press Club, the venality and bickering were there, but there was something else there as well. The buildings embodied a human adventure. The soldiers in the streets provoked this knowledge. There was danger in how men cared about their lives. Robert felt a kind of awe in the face of this.

He walked into the lobby of the Centre Block and told a security guard his business. The man made a phone call and gave him directions. Robert took an elevator and followed long halls until he came to the office. The door was open. Peter was sitting behind a desk.

Peter rose and came to the door of the office to meet him, his hand extended, face smiling, a man almost as tall as Robert himself, but heavier, the vest of his dark suit curving smoothly over the beginnings of a paunch, echoing the curves of his developing jowl and balding head. He was smooth and substantial.

"Hello old man, good to see you again, would you like

coffee?" It all came out in one long clearly articulated sentence.

"Yes," Robert said, "I would." He felt uneasy as he stood there shaking hands, as if he had blundered into the office of a stranger and claimed kinship.

"I tried to phone you the last time I was through Kingston," Peter said, "but I couldn't get hold of you. Dorothy and I have often spoken of you recently and meant to write and get you up for the weekend, but we've simply neglected it for too long. So I was very pleased when you called. I'll just go and get us some coffee."

He went out a side door into an adjoining office where a secretary was typing. Robert sat nervously in the chair and looked around the room. On the wall was a faded print of a painting by Tom Thomson, and behind the desk was a picture of Dorothy with three children, two girls in their teens and a baby boy. Robert hadn't seen Dorothy for years and the face in the photograph was like a mask made to resemble the girl he had known in university, the same fine wide smile that made her seem more open and spontaneous than she ever was. Dorothy had been a girl on the way up, in fact that was the reason why although she and Robert had gone out a few times, there had never been anything serious between them, for Robert had been, even then, unpredictable and moody, not someone to be counted on.

He looked back at Dorothy's face, at the faces of the children, frozen, empty. There was nothing wrong with the faces in the photograph except what was wrong with the faces in all studio photographs: they were informed by an inadequate mythology. All those hundreds of photographers were at best craftsmen expressing empty myths. Karsh, with his varnished faces of the famous, was simply a more expensive expression of the same thing.

There was an echo of Dorothy's face in the face of the younger daughter. Once he had spoken to Dorothy, kissed her but she had a different face then. Or did she? Had he kissed this ugly icon? He shuddered and thought of Elizabeth. Was there one inevitable mask that her face would become or did she have some choice? He had the sense of her beautiful face as a mask covering a hideous deformity, her inevitable future.

"Do you take cream and sugar?" Peter called out from the next room.

"Yes, please," Robert said. He was suddenly conscious that the room had no window. He wanted to see the sky. How could a man make decisions about what was good for a constituency or a country in a room where he couldn't see the sky?

Peter walked into the room with two cups of coffee in his hands. The cups were plastic of an unpleasant green colour.

"Here we are, Robert. I'm lucky, by the way, to share the services of a secretary who makes very good coffee."

He passed Robert one cup and sat down in the chair opposite him.

"Well, how is everything, Robert? We were sorry to hear that you and Jenny had split up, but of course it may be the best thing for both of you. One finds it hard to guess these days."

"I'm managing. I think Jenny is too."

"You're with the university press now."

Robert nodded. He was being interviewed, and the situation amused him. He was tempted to spill Peter's coffee all over him and see if that could disturb his composure: what did the perfect political gentleman do when he had hot coffee poured on his balls?

Why was he angry at Peter? He was here because they were supposed to be friends.

"Sometimes," Robert said, "I'm tempted to go back into commercial publishing, even go back to England, but I think my plans will work themselves out there. How are things with you?"

"Good, I think. It's not always easy to tell. I'm ambitious, Robert, and not all that young, but I've only been in Parliament two years. I know how to work on committees, and I'm a good constituency man. I get my people what they need. I have some weight in the caucus."

The speech suddenly seemed familiar to Robert, he remembered the kind of confidence that Peter had always had when he faced a set of practical problems, the way he could analyze and define, nearly always find something in himself that could confront and solve whatever was in front of him. As he moved from sentence to sentence, one could sense the discrimination with which he observed himself and his situation. No wonder he was a fine lawyer.

They looked at each other without speaking, Peter's hazel eyes, with only a few wrinkles at the edges, holding very still, unblinking.

"I guess it's been very strange in Ottawa the last three weeks."

"I was tempted to send Dorothy and the children away, but I suppose that was just panic."

"There's been a lot of panic in everybody's reaction."

Peter looked at him without answering. Something in the tone of Robert's remark had silenced him. Robert wished once more that the room had a window. He felt surrounded, but he had to go on talking. Maybe the book was a safe subject.

"That's what I came to see you about," he said. "This whole kidnapping crisis, the War Measures Act, all of it. I'd like to do a book about it. Eye-witness reports, but from people who only saw things from a distance. A kind of set of diaries of the time, with all the history between the lines."

Peter watched, nodded.

"I thought you might be interested in doing some kind of report from here, assessing things that are in the background of the government's reaction as you saw it. And just tell how it felt."

"I don't yet know how it feels. I keep thinking about Pierre Laporte's children. It's disgusting. I don't like to have to think about it."

"We have to think about it."

"No. We just have to get it over."

"Is that really what you think?"

"Yes."

"Then you approve of the War Measures Act?"

"It's clear from the way you ask that you don't."

"I don't see how anyone could."

"It was necessary, Robert, believe me."

"Why?"

"Many reasons. Some are obvious, some are secret."

"None of them is obvious to me. And no government that claims to be democratic can act on the basis of secret information and still make that claim."

"That's childish, Robert."

"No, it isn't. Not at all."

"Do you really think that we can just tell everybody everything?"

"Secrecy begets corruption."

"Yes, I know... and all power tends to corrupt."

"At least you got it right."

"He was joking."

"I don't trust that kind of joke, Peter. Look, don't the implications of the War Measures Act bother you?"

"I'm not that much of a theorist. It's a weapon. We use it and then put it away. Ordinary people understand that."

The horror to Robert was that this might be true.

"This isn't a perfect democracy," Peter went on, "and no-one with any sense believes one will ever exist. When a good man is strangled and his body left in a car trunk as some kind of gesture, most ordinary people want reassurance. They want to know where they stand."

"You weren't always so skeptical about political theory."

"Robert, the answer to that is too obvious to give. It would be an insult to assume you don't know it."

"Unlike you, I've never grown up."

"I don't know. We haven't seen much of each other for a long time. You do seem a purist."

"Perhaps so. I know in a way that none of it matters. We're in the hands of the big money, politics is a game they allow us to play. But we can't turn our backs on history just because we can't control it."

"Deep down, you're still some kind of Marxist, Robert. There are no concrete universals for me. History is just a record of what happened. Civilization is the record of how men have got free of that. It all just goes on, from day to day, with a few individual men, whatever happens, learning to be civilized."

"And to have a house in Rockcliffe, a polite wife and three children."

"It's less fashionable than divorce, I suppose. I can see what your picture of me must be. Anything to get closer to the centre of power."

"Did I say that?"

"No. But you thought it, I imagine."

"Let's say it's one of those painful half-truths that we all have to live with."

Peter was silent, looking at the wall then turning to Robert. His eyes were hurt.

"You were never an easy friend, Robert. That's part of why I value your friendship. I must say I don't know how Jenny stood you all those years."

"Neither do I."

"I can't write the piece for you. It wouldn't be what you want, would it?"

"No."

"There are some other people here I could introduce you to."

Now it was Robert's turn to stare at the wall. Somewhere near the door of the Parliament Buildings Elizabeth was waiting for him. She was young and pretty and didn't care what happened in Parliament or on the streets. He could go down and tell her to wait and then he could search out others, perhaps someone in the NDP, who would give him the kind of essay he wanted. She would be bored, would watch people go by, take a few photographs. While he tried to go part of the way back to the years when he had commissioned books, spent hours drinking with writers as they made vast plans and reduced those plans to possibilities.

"No, Peter, I think I'll let it go. For today anyway. I'll phone you if I change my mind."

"Let's have lunch then."

"Another time Peter. Thanks for seeing me."

"I'm not too ambitious to have no time for old friends, not yet anyway."

Robert stood up, and they shook hands.

10

Most of an atom is nothing, where had she learned that? But she had always known something like that in the moments when she only saw the spaces between things. Her head grew tight, as if in a band of silver, and as she looked out the windows, she could say the words, field, grass, weed stems, purple wild asters, but she knew them only after she had said their names. In themselves they were nothing; she could only see the spaces between, where they went dead.

Repeat the facts like a litany: I am in a car with Robert. He is angry with me, but if I talk with him, he will come back. Perhaps. The car is dark green. In front of me, dashboard, glove compartment, silver lettering. As I ought to have my name on my forehead in silver lettering so that I could touch it with my fingers and know who I am in silver. I am in a car with Robert. Perhaps I love him sometimes, but he is a space between my thoughts and my hands now. He is angry with me.

She looked out the window. There were trees beside the road and their leaves were many colours, and oddly lit as the afternoon sun shone between them. These are leaves. Probably they are beautiful. She wanted to talk to Robert so that he would not be angry, would talk about things and make them real. He would tell her about the leaves, that they were beautiful, and then she would know.

Elizabeth closed her eyes and hated him. A band of silver came inside her head and pressed outward. Why did she have to speak first? It was too much. She couldn't do it. If he spoke to her, she would love him for knowing her need. Meanwhile she hated him.

In Ottawa, as they had walked along the streets, she had been afraid that she would meet her mother. A dozen times she had met her mother's face and seen the expression. What was it? What was her mother feeling? At first Elizabeth thought that it was anger, that black raging stillness that she had seen before, when no-one could speak to help her. Or was that true?

The look was not anger. She imagined her mother walking toward them along the street, not noticing until a few seconds after Elizabeth had seen her and begun to shake. Her head turned and she looked straight into Elizabeth's eyes and saw nothing. That curious moment when she looked at her as if she were a stranger, and Elizabeth saw her mother as truly as if she were dead, and then the face knew her.

Fear, panic, that's what it was. Her daughter keeping secrets from her, travelling secretly with a man 40 years old. It must be wrong or it wouldn't be a secret. Elizabeth often wondered about that, why she hadn't told her mother about Robert. She could say that her mother wouldn't understand, but that answered nothing.

To do what was right, to be seen to do what was right, to be the Good Daughter, always. Now she was not, now she was falling into the space of nothing that was within each atom. She hated Robert for taking her there, hated the tall body that hunched over the wheel in his angry silence.

Still she knew that she could never quite be the Good Daughter. They hadn't taught her enough of the rules, something like that. You asked about things, and they said, it will go away, it's not what you really feel deep down.

Martha had understood. They would wake in the morning in each other's arms and go through their litany, "What did you dream?" "What does it mean?" "What shall we do today?"

Elizabeth was fourteen, Martha a few months older, and during that summer at the cottage Martha had stayed with them for six weeks. She and Elizabeth had a cabin to themselves with two single beds in it, but every night they would climb into bed together because the cabin was chilly in the evening, and they would talk and then fall asleep in each other's arms.

Elizabeth had reached almost her full height; Martha was shorter and heavier, and her breasts were already large and soft. Elizabeth's were still small and pointed, and sometimes as they lay there in bed together, she would feel Martha's heaviness against her and wonder if she would develop like that.

Mornings they would wake into the bright summer light and go through their list of questions, then get up from the bed and watch each other dress, and it was always odd because they felt they were one person but they looked so different and would laugh to see the illusion of their separateness.

As the summer went on, their bodies grew familiar, loving and hesitant. There was never anything between them like this electric silence between her and Robert. Men were such children. Even with Tom, who was so gentle and amenable, there had been a strangeness that chilled her sometimes. She could love him only in the dark, and even then it was a gift given from a distance. She lay there miles below him.

When she and Martha talked, each seemed to be inside the skin of the other. Elizabeth would look out across the lake, through the maze of rocks that formed the channel, and she would see Martha on water-skis, so far away that the motorboat was almost silent, and Elizabeth would know what Martha was thinking. At first, sometimes, she would ask, but soon she knew that she would always be right.

Elizabeth was so far back in her own mind now, so lost in the emptiness between the electrons of her thought, that she was afraid to open her eyes. If she saw the light, she would grow dizzy and faint.

She sat with her eyes closed and listened to the steady sound of the engine, felt the hum of the car wheels on the road rising through her spine and into her head. If she could concentrate hard enough on this, it would be safe to open her eyes.

Tomorrow she would take the whole morning to write to Martha. Martha's recent letters from England had been odd and fragmentary, but still, from time to time, she would put words to something that was in Elizabeth's mind. *Women are creatures from outer space or inner time. Only a new science fiction can tell about us.* That in a recent letter. Yes, Elizabeth thought when she read it, and again now, yes, that is the truth. Sometime when she felt very close to Robert she would call him Earthman and see if he understood.

She hated him. No-one else could cut into her being like that. Martha had once been inside her gently and completely, Tom had bumped against her, awkward, childish, in need of comfort. But Robert was armed with knives.

Elizabeth was becoming frightened again and opened her eyes. She was dizzy for a moment, but got hold of herself.

"Were you asleep?" Robert said.

"No," she said. "Just thinking."

The car moved up a hill past another piece of woods where the leaves seemed to contain the slanting sunlight. Elizabeth was looking into the depth of the woods when she heard Robert make a sound that was something between a curse and a gasp. Events went out of sequence. Her hand flew out, hurt when it struck the dashboard. The car slid sideways. The brakes screamed. The dark shape of another car moved out of sight. A sound came from her that was almost a scream.

When time came back together they were coming to a stop on the shoulder of the road and her wrist ached.

"Are you all right?" Robert said. His face seemed blurred. She nodded.

"My wrist hurts, but it's nothing serious."

Robert put his arms on the steering wheel and his head on top of them. He was silent, but Elizabeth could see that his chest was heaving rhythmically in great silent sobs of breath that terrified her. She wanted not to see him, and she turned her head away, but the sight of him drew her back. Gradually his breathing grew slower and shallower, but Elizabeth could not bear the pressure, until suddenly, like something breaking, he seemed small and hurt, a child, and she leaned across the seat and stroked the back of his head, then moved to him and put her arms around him. His body was shaking as if chilled, and Elizabeth was surprised that she hadn't been more frightened. For her it had simply been a strange break in the pattern of time, a pain going up her arm and then everything still again. Probably because she hadn't been driving, hadn't been in control.

Robert lifted his head and looked toward her, his face grey and the eyes lost somewhere. Her anger seemed strange now he was so close and weak. She felt that she could carry him through the world, that she loved him terribly. He kissed her on the cheek and held his head against her.

"We're alive by three inches," he said.

"We're alive."

"I can hardly believe it."

"We are. We're alive."

"In the middle of that, while I was hanging onto the wheel trying to hold us on the road and miss that other car, there was a strange moment when I thought I was dead. I was outside myself and flying or floating. It must be the moment when the adrenalin hit. I felt free, completely free, not even worried."

As they talked, he had stopped shaking, and now he lifted his head away from her and breathed deeply.

He stroked her hair.

"How's your wrist?"

"It hurts."

"Let me look."

She held it out to him. His long fingers took hold of it and felt it gently. It hurt when he squeezed the joint. He lifted her hand and kissed the edge of it. Just then the car was shaken by the air currents from a large truck that drove quickly past them.

"We'd better get going," Robert said, "before someone runs into us and finishes the job."

Elizabeth meant to move away, but instead stayed close beside him on the seat. As she watched his hands reach out to turn the key, move to the transmission, then to the steering wheel, she felt curiously as if they were caressing her, almost as if they moved inside her.

"What happened back there?" she said as the car pulled away. "I didn't really see."

"There was a car coming from the other direction and trying to pass too close to the hill. When we came over the brow of the hill he was coming straight at me. I think I missed him by just a few inches. Don't like to think about it."

Everything was different now, had altered its shape. She could talk to him.

"You were angry." Elizabeth said.

"I was scared."

"No. Before. Until then."

"It didn't go very well with Peter."

"But you were angry with me."

"I didn't like the Mr. and Mrs. Tourist routine."

"I knew you wouldn't."

"That's why you did it."

"I like snapshots, they help me remember things."

"So that you can evade the present."

Elizabeth could feel herself slipping away from him again.

He reached out and put his hand on her leg.

"Let's not fight," he said. "I'll forget about the snapshot. It shouldn't be important after coming so close to getting killed."

She looked toward him, and saw that his face was still pale. Here eyes examined the wrinkles that were beginning on his face, and the pattern of his beard. She wondered how he would look if he grew the beard.

"Have you ever grown a beard?" she said.

"No. I think the whiskers are too thin. Besides I'm the kind of person who'd find he had things living in it. Like the old man in the limerick."

"I've never kissed a man with a beard."

"Neither have I."

Elizabeth turned to him and kissed his cheek.

"I like you," she said.

"Good. But don't kiss the driver while the car is in motion."

Elizabeth sat back and looked at the road unwinding ahead of them. In spite of the danger they had just passed, she felt safe. They were alone together in the car as if they could drive on through the whole world like this. They sat in their places, she sat on his right, and they watched the darkness coming up out of the earth. The car seemed to be going faster as darkness fell, as if together they were outrunning the night and all the ghostly pursuers of the night. It was all right now, she could touch him. Her shoulder was against his as they travelled into the city.

From the top of the hill at Barriefield, the city was bright and exciting. It was her home now; she was closer to herself here than she had been in Ottawa.

She and Robert were entering the city together and lights shone to greet them. Then they disappeared into the familiar streets, moving along the earth as the cathedral reached above them and the old houses looked down on them. Robert drove to her apartment, the headlights catching and passing the lovers in the evening streets. It was the time of year for lovers, the green world dying, the young holding their bodies together against the cold. Most of an atom is nothing; dance then, hold your lover.

They got out of the car in silence, moved as if tranced, toward the room above. When they entered, it was dark except for the light from the street, and Elizabeth did not turn on the light, only closed the door and reached to hold Robert against her. She felt brave, defiant, watched him taking off his clothes in the half light, seeing every angle of bone and flesh. She held him and they fell toward the bed.

As they moved together on the bed, she thought of buildings and trees towering above them, and stars above those, a huge high flowering of space, and the two of them, tiny, tiny, far away below it. As his excitement grew, he urged her on, demanding that she come with him, his teeth and fingernails rousing her to the surface of her skin. She was losing him, and they seemed tiny and cold, and her hips moved with a desperation to reach him, but it was like a race she was watching. What he wanted was to destroy her. He wanted her to die for him. She would not. He went on and on, without her. She tried to vanish into her body for him, and when she failed, she hurt him in his pleasure and panted with the joy of this power.

11

I was set the task of learning from the patient something that I did not know and that he did not know himself. I take that as my text, brothers and sisters, fathers and prophets. After the Subtle Doctor, the Angelic Doctor, all the others, we move on to this text from the Secular Doctor, the Courageous Doctor. I have a wife who is not my wife. A young girl whose body I enter as if it were an unnatural act. I had thought that only a woman who could understand me could create me.

Robert walked through the front door of Gavin's school. He regretted his promise to Gavin that he would attend the concert. He had wanted Elizabeth to come with him but she had refused, and they had argued about it. Elizabeth would not recognize how much easier it would be for him with her at his side. The eyes that seized him would do less harm.

Robert entered the school gym and took a seat. Across the aisle from him, he noticed Craig Wardell, the alderman. Wardell was almost too smartly dressed. Ambition shone like a kind of light on his skin, but he had the wrong style for a city the size of Kingston. His wife was a pretty, tall girl with protruberant teeth. They both smiled and nodded, from time to time, to other parents who filed into the gymnasium and placed themselves on the rows of straight chairs.

Directly in front of Robert's chair sat a small woman in her sixties who was wearing a shabby coat and holding a large imitation-leather purse. A ten-year-old girl sat with her, twisting constantly in her chair to see everything that happened, and the old woman would turn to her from time to time and, whispering loudly, would tell her to sit still.

The little girl turned and stared at him. She had a fat face, pale blue eyes with thin lashes. Robert smiled at her, but she didn't react, just turned away.

As the seats around him began to get full, Robert felt the

edges of a panic that sometimes seized him in crowds, a kind of shiver moving across his forehead, over his shoulder blades. He'd taken a seat on the aisle and not too far from the door, but still he felt oppressed by the manyness of the strangers. He wanted to be invisible, not to be there, or to have Elizabeth beside him to keep him safe. His stomach began to hurt. He looked toward the door and saw Barbara Walker standing there, her head tilted a little back as if the fine bones of her face were stinging with awareness. She was Jennifer's best friend in Kingston, a beautiful woman whose husband was constantly and notoriously unfaithful to her, but who seemed never to react directly to this, only to be more and more beautiful as the attack of light and air moulded her fine bones.

She saw Robert and raised her gloved hand in greeting. He would have signalled to her to sit with him, but at that moment a large family came in from the other end of the row and took all the seats. Barbara took a seat in the crowded area near the front. The gymnasium was almost full now, and the sound of voices had reached the level of a sustained murmur. Now and then a single voice or a laugh would rise above the even tenor of the hubbub.

Several minutes after the hour, the principal came out from behind the curtains and stood at the edge of the stage to welcome them. He was a tall man, with big hands, who stood there slightly stooped, talking in a voice that still had an echo of the country in it. He looked as if he would have been more comfortable as the school janitor. Though he appeared to accept the series of accidents that had placed him in front of this crowd, he was untouched by them. Near the front door of the gym stood a couple of the other men teachers, clean-cut young men, presentable, shining. Robert knew that they would teach efficiently. He disliked them. He preferred the older man on the platform who seemed to rock slightly as he spoke and went on slowly, carefully mouthing pointless phrases until he felt that he had said enough, then retired behind the stage curtain.

The noise of voices in the auditorium started up again. Nothing happened. Outside the gym doors, in the hall, there was a certain amount of movement back and forth.

After several minutes the stage curtains opened part way, revealing half of the kindergarten rhythm band. The curtains stuck. The middle-aged kindergarten teacher gestured to someone backstage. The teacher at the piano made a similar gesture. Someone in the rhythm band waved to a suddenly visible parent. A flashbulb went off.

After a delay of a minute or two, during which there were several minor mutinies among band members, the principal came to the edge of the curtain. He took it in his hand and led it offstage. One of the newly revealed band members waved. They came to some sort of attention as their leader, a small fat girl in a pink dress, raised her baton.

The piano began to march. The rhythm band followed. The miniature leader beat time with vengeful authority. After a few minutes it all stopped and the audience applauded. Robert had stopped smoking three years before, but suddenly he was desperate for a cigarette. He shifted in his seat and looked at his watch, then did some rough calculations of how long it would take to reach the Grade Six choir. He began to wonder how Gavin would feel if no-one was there to see him perform.

The school principal came out to the centre of the stage and explained that the curtain didn't seem to be working properly. He explained why. It was a matter of the poor mounting of a pulley. He had thought of trying to repair it, but it seemed better to leave the curtain open for the whole performance. However the Grade Eight boys' woodworking class had offered to look into it. Still it seemed best to leave the curtain open.

As he walked off the stage, the curtain closed. Someone in the audience applauded. A tall embarrassed boy walked to the edge of the curtain and pulled it open again. Several people applauded. Another rhythm band came on the stage. This, the teacher at the piano announced, was the afternoon kindergarten. The other had been the morning kindergarten. Robert closed his eyes and pretended he was dead. He imagined Elizabeth's naked body and succeeded in giving himself an erection, which seemed somehow to change the balance of chemicals in his body and make him able to ignore the next ten minutes of the concert.

His attention returned as the Grade Two choir sang "The Happy Wanderer." He focused on a small boy whose face was lit up with sheer joy in singing, especially on the ah-ah-ha-ha-ha. His head was back and moved from side to side with the music's rhythm.

Valder ah-ha-ha-ha-ha-ha.

Next came two girls in green suits with spangles who tap-danced to a worn record of "Deep in the Heart of Texas."

The Grade Three choir: "Molly Malone" and "The Age of Aquarius." At the end of each number, a few parents went out to meet their children and leave. Robert wondered how many would be left by the end of the concert.

He found himself unable to sit still, shifting from one buttock to the other, turning sideways with his feet in the aisle, crossing and uncrossing his long legs, which were starting to ache from being folded into a space too small for them. He tried to watch Barbara where she sat a dozen rows in front of him. She seemed to sit perfectly still. How many inner deaths had to take place before such poise was possible? For the first time he was aware of Barbara as a woman he wanted. Before this, her beautiful face had always seemed unreal, something to be admired from a distance, but the sudden feeling of the disasters that must take place daily in her soul made her solid and desirable.

The choir finished, and a group of parents got up to leave. The next group filed in, a choir, three girls with recorders and a boy with a drum. Robert stood and walked to the door.

When he got outside, he stood still, taking deep breaths of the cold air. His body expanded, became gigantic. He looked at his watch, discovered that it was only 45 minutes since he had entered the building. It seemed like hours.

He remembered once sitting in a dentist's chair during the long painful extraction of a wisdom tooth, remembered noticing that his mouth felt huge, as if the dentist could walk in, hand in hand with his nurse, accompanied, if necessary, by cranes, bulldozers, a crew of men with picks and shovels.

He must, he supposed, wait and go back to the concert. He had told Gavin he would be there; still the boy knew that he was moody and unreliable. He couldn't go back in, have those who had seen him leave watch curiously as he returned.

As he stood in the schoolyard, a car went by, then the streets were empty. The night was cloudy, and the sky above him was a nebulous darkness. He shivered and reached in his pocket for the car keys.

Tomorrow he would phone Gavin and explain it all to him. Part of growing up was learning to accept other people's weaknesses. The boy would have to face that.

As Robert got into the car and started the engine, he wondered where he was going. He started to drive, without deciding, thinking that there was something magic about a car at night moving through dark streets. Something hidden, like a thought moving along the dark corridors of the brain. Laporte's body driven through the city. Hidden in the trunk of a car. The soldiers moved through the dark streets. Secret. He was driving past the university, saw students move in and out of the library, in and out of the union and the gym. The streets here were open. Open streets and secret streets. Secret when the city became a map of the brain. A corpse in the trunk of a car moving through the streets of the just city.

He parked his car just down the street from Elizabeth's apartment. He was glad to be here. Their argument had been foolish, pointless.

When he reached the door of her apartment, he heard a man's voice, the voice of Wayne Burtch. Robert couldn't be

fair or decent, it made him furious. He had no resiliency left
for sharing Elizabeth with her friend, who was in fact a hang-
dog lover, waiting futilely for her to notice him.

What he should do, Robert knew, was walk away, go back
to his apartment and phone if he wanted to talk to her. He
knocked on the door.

Elizabeth answered, smiling and intimate, and somehow
impersonal. Their eyes met, and he felt he wanted to drive hers
back into her head, to make her explode with the energy of
his anger and desire. He nodded to Wayne, wanting him to
leave. He gave no sign of getting the message. He was sitting
on the edge of the bed, leaning sideways over a pillow. Robert
sat down at the other end.

Wayne was wearing blue jeans and a university jacket. They
made him look heavier, bulkier. Robert hated him.

"Do you think I shouldn't move back home, Lizzie?" the
younger man said. "I feel really good since I decided to go."

"Then I guess you should. I don't know why I can't get used
to the idea."

"Did I tell you I got a postcard from Pam?"

"No. Where is she?"

"She was in London. It's a picture of Henry the Eighth from
the National Portrait Gallery. She says he looks like me."

"That was mean."

"Oh, I didn't take it seriously."

Robert listened in silence. They were doing it on purpose,
leaving him out; he was old, he didn't know their friends.
Elizabeth turned to him.

"How was it?" she said.

"Okay."

"What?" Burtch said.

"Nothing important."

Burtch went on talking about people Robert didn't know.
It was a vicious little game. Robert looked at Elizabeth to see
how she was taking it, but she avoided his eyes. It went on

Robert sat on his anger like a broody hen on a clutch of hand grenades. He was almost beginning to enjoy it. His silence was gaining ground against their conversation. The breaks in their speech were longer. At last the conversation died, and Burtch got up to leave. Robert looked out the window and waited for him to be gone. The door closed behind him.

"That was a pretty scene," he said as he heard the heavy footsteps go down the stairs.

"What was?"

"The two of you ignoring me."

"We weren't. You were just quiet."

"Your innocence is charming."

She went and sat down in the chair, her face turned away from him.

"If you want that chunky young man, then you should make that decision, and not keep me hanging around."

The telephone rang. Elizabeth picked it up, recognized the voice and smiled.

"Hi," she said. "I just wrote you a letter yesterday. With a note in it for Philip."

Robert stood up and walked out of the room, closing the door quietly behind him. He wanted to slam it, to leave some mark on her conversation with her mother, but there was no point. When he got outside, he walked to the car and got in. He drove at random around several blocks, out Brock Street and back down Princess.

I get in my car, Elizabeth. I participate in all the pointless movement of this city. Who are you to do this to me? I will drive down a dozen streets until my anger abates and then I will return to you, the stillness of your face, your room. Who are you to do this to me?

Robert turned the wheels of the car toward his own apartment. He would not go back to her, instead would cling to the decency of his solitude. Now that it was too late, he regretted not having waited for Gavin's class choir.

Safely alone in his apartment, Robert made himself a drink. On the desk was the most recent of Marion's letters suggesting that he come to Toronto and visit their father. The old man was not recovering after the stroke, and there were signs of a weakening of the heart. Robert had ignored Marion's suggestion long enough. She was right; perhaps neither of them liked the old man, but they must acknowledge him. He decided to go within the next week.

Robert turned on the little television set in front of his chair and let a police show happen in front of him. After his second drink, he began to feel almost contented, feeling a kind of nostalgia for the solitary days before he had met Elizabeth. They were so simple.

When the phone rang, he knew it was Elizabeth, and a part of him wanted not to answer.

"I'm sorry Robert," she said. It always moved him to hear her speak his name.

"I suppose I'm not very patient," he said.

"I was upset when I saw you walking out, and I saw the look on your face, but I couldn't just hang up on my mother. Could I?"

"I guess not," he said, not meaning it.

" How was the concert?"

"I left before Gavin's class sang."

"Why?"

"I started to get claustrophobic. They're always ridiculous, those concerts."

"Are you going to come over?" Her voice was soft, pleading.

"I'm a bit tired."

"Can I come over there? I need a walk."

"Sure. I'd like that."

12

Sometimes the book was a diary, but at other times it was something else, a record of thoughts or perceptions. Sometimes it held things together and sometimes it dispersed them.

Colours: blue, white, grey, mauve sometimes, a few greens, e.g., the colour of a field of young oats. The whites and greys of the snow on Mount Robson towering beside the train coming back from Vancouver that summer. The pastel colours of the breasts of the mourning doves I used to see on the road by Grandpa's farm. There should be more names for blue. My father's eyes, the lake on a summer day, bachelor's buttons, iris, the sky before dark, the dress with ruffled sleeves I had when I was twelve.

Elizabeth took out her photograph album and opened it, glancing at the pictures, not so much at the subjects as at the colours. They were schematic, most of them, red, blue, green. She had seen professional pictures that were different from this, but hers presented a simple world. Sometimes she liked them best when they were a little out of focus, when the camera seemed to have tried to capture someone but had failed.

She turned back to the front of the book. It contained pictures of her parents, some from before she was born; once going through an old box of family photographs, she had seen these and asked her mother for them. In these pictures, her father was young and handsome, and her mother young and happy. They were always smiling. There was a picture of them both standing on the dock at the cottage with the rowboat floating at their feet at the edge of the patch of reeds. There was a newspaper picture of her father when he had been named secretary to an important government commission. There was a picture of them with their arms around each other on their twentieth wedding anniversary. It was when Elizabeth was sixteen, and she remembered her Aunt Beth asking her help in making the arrangements for the party. She remembered the dance at the club, her mother and father dancing together and everyone applauding.

Their life made sense. It has a line of development. Her father's career, her parents' companionable marriage, went forward according to some kind of plan. The photographs seemed like moments stolen out of a significant progress. She recognized what she saw as life.

What happened to her never quite made sense in this way. It all failed to come together. Once she had thought it was only a matter of being young, that she would grow to the age when things would make sense, would marry, everything would happen as it should. But that had not yet happened, and now it seemed farther away than ever. Now this curious monster, desire, that Robert had brought to birth in her, performed its erratic dance through her life. It was at odds with everything. Sometimes he was cruel to her. By all the rules it ought to end there, but it went on, became more complicated. It was not what she wanted. She felt the edge of something crowd her, threaten her. A moment breathless and big with fear. Or was it possibility?

Robert would never fit into a progress like the one she had seen in her parents' life, in her grandparents'. She thought of the houses on her street at home. The Wallaces, the MacEwans, the Undercrofts. A red brick, a yellow brick, a white frame. Tom's house around the corner. She should have married Tom, borne his baby. She had missed her chance for that kind of life, for a life that joined the lives of her family, continued in the familiar way. The child would have been four years old now; she imagined a child in the room with her and shivered. The ghost child refused to go away. It stood in the corner of the room staring at her. It had a monstrous head and was still in diapers though it was far too old.

It had come out of her body. The doctor had probed her more deeply than she had thought possible. He had torn some-

134

thing in her, something he didn't know or care that he had touched. She had curled up in the back seat like a child beginning to grow. She would grow back whatever it was she had lost. It was not clear to her if she had healed herself or only avoided seeing the wound, but now Robert had started the bleeding again. He went into her too far, tore something deep in her guts.

To think of him in her, his blunt mute tool opening her, was comic or absurd. She could not imagine wanting that of all things. It was not beautiful, it made no sense.

She turned the page of the photo album. Herself, a baby, with a round, serious face, held in her mother's arms. I am. I am. I am. She closed her eyes and let her mind go back in time to find herself somewhere. She could remember a room in sunlight with a toy animal that was red and yellow. There was an adult, but she did not know who it could be. Not her mother, perhaps her father. There was some kind of presence, a sort of emotional shadow on the memory, but she could not find an explanation.

Elizabeth looked at her watch and wondered what Robert was doing. He had planned to take his children somewhere for lunch. He had wanted her to go along, but she could not. It was too foreign to her. Now she turned the pages of the book, looking at photographs as if they were pictures of someone else. At thirteen with Martha, grinning absurdly.

Would Martha understand what she was feeling? She turned a page and saw Tom, who had never understood anything yet was gentle. She wondered if that was only because he was young then. The last time she had seen him, she had looked at his face and thought that there was something new in it, perhaps something harder. Did the ghost child leave marks on him as well?

Robert sat hunched in a leather chair, nervously running his head against the back of it. He told himself that it was none

135

of his affair if the house was a mess, but still it annoyed him; it was a physical thing, like the taste of oil. Tensed, he looked around him and saw the desk covered with papers, the empty juice glasses on the TV set, a pillow lying over the hall chair. That and the comic books everywhere. He couldn't for a moment understand why Jennifer let Gavin leave his comics lying around like that. Still, it was none of his business. His presence in the house was an accident; he had no more rights here than a repairman.

When Jennifer had told him she might not be back until after four, he hadn't thought much about it, expecting that after he and the children had had lunch at the old Lakeside Hotel, they would walk for a while, down the gravel road that crossed the mill dam and along past the Seven Cottages and at least as far as the point where the road curved down to the lake and there was a boat ramp. Both the children liked walking, and it was something he could share with them in an easy way.

But then Cindy had got sick at the hotel. They were sitting at lunch in the large empty room, only the three of them among the empty red-and-white chairs and tables. It was the last weekend the hotel was open. They sat waiting for their food and talked about the stuffed fish on the walls, how unreal they looked when they were mounted, their skins varnished, and their mouths open in a stylized gesture of predation. Their teeth showed but seemed like nothing that a living creature could possess. The fish had the shine and empty glamour of a false boast.

The food was brought, a chicken casserole that was always good at the Lakeside, but Cindy had eaten only a few bites when she sat back in her chair, her face pale and frightened, lips compressed.

"I don't feel very well," she said.

"What's the matter?" Robert said.

"I don't know, Daddy. I just feel sick."

Suddenly she stood up, knocking over her wooden chair, and began to run from the room, her hand over her mouth. Robert followed her. As she reached the outside door, she turned to her left for one or two steps, then bent and vomited into the dark earth of the garden. Robert stood at the top of the steps and watched her; best to leave her alone until it was over. How slight and yet how womanly she looked, even at this moment when her body betrayed her.

She stood for a moment breathing deeply with her forehead in her hands, her yellow blouse bright against the faded clapboard of the hotel. Dead chrysanthemums rose beside her; beyond, the lake reflected the grey sky, the branches of drowned trees reached upward like the fingers of an underwater darkness that had been petrified by the contact with light. Below he imagined a forest of monstrosities curling away downward where fish with sharp teeth hung still in the space of the water, then rushed to attack and devour. On the bare earth, his daughter's vomit spread its coloured bits like an ornament. His child, earth's ornament. She must be cold in the wind in only a thin blouse. Robert walked to the girl and put his hand on her shoulder.

"I'm sorry Daddy."

"No need to be. You're sick. Let's go to the car, and you can wrap up in a blanket while I drive you home."

"We can still go for our walk. I'll feel better in a minute."

"You must be coming down with something. I'd better take you home."

He held his arm around her shoulders as they walked to the car. She felt light and weak. She got in the back seat while Robert opened the trunk and took out a plaid blanket he kept in there. He wrapped it around her, started the motor and put on the heater. Then he walked back toward the hotel to get Gavin.

As he walked into the dining-room, he saw that Gavin was eating enthusiastically, nearly finished his main course.

"Cindy's sick, Gavin. I think we'd better drive her home."

"Aren't you going to eat your dinner? I'm still hungry."

"I'll get you a chocolate bar on the way out," Robert said. "That will do you instead of dessert."

"Okay," Gavin said. "What's wrong with Cindy?"

"I don't know. Some kind of 'flu maybe."

Robert stopped to pay the bill on the way out and had to explain twice why he was leaving without eating his meal. The woman at the desk, determined to be friendly, asked if Cindy wanted to lie down in the back room. Robert insisted that he only wanted to take her home. He bought a chocolate bar for Gavin and one for himself. He knew he would soon start to get hungry.

They had walked to the car and driven back to town, Cindy lying shivering in the seat even after the car had become quite warm, Gavin sitting beside him in the front, making conversation in a rather obvious way. Robert liked the boy for his determination to be cheerful and sociable through this minor emergency. Gavin had often got on his nerves over the years, but driving along this highway, it seemed to Robert that the boy would grow up to be a good man.

Halfway back it had started to rain heavily, and Gavin had stopped talking, as if the sound of rain had made speech unnecessary. They drove along, the rain and the windshield wipers talking rhythmically to them.

Now Cindy lay on her bed upstairs with a hot-water bottle, and Gavin had retreated to the basement where he was working on a school project at the desk in the corner where Robert had once spent many hours. Robert sat down in an old leather chair that had always been a favourite of his. When he had moved out, he'd taken very little furniture with him, partly because he hadn't wanted to discuss the whole question with Jennifer, and partly because he had felt the need to simplify his life, to live in the kind of stripped down, barren surroundings that had since oppressed him. But now that Elizabeth had become part of his life, he was beginning to want to furnish his world again, and to shape the furnishing around her. Was it the need to tie her to his life with things, with objects they shared? Because he was afraid that she would leave him, that she would grow tired of him and want a simpler man, a happier, younger, more innocent man? Robert got up from the chair, frightened by the thought of Elizabeth leaving him, seeing him plain at last and finding a better man. He knew he was a man neither strong nor good, but when he looked around him at the other men of his acquaintance, they seemed equally foolish. Perhaps his anger gave him some kind of reality. He walked nervously around the room, standing to look for a moment into the grey afternoon, then turning and walking again.

He stood by the desk for a moment looking down at the paper, and he noticed an English air letter. It was addressed to a man who had been dead for several years. Mr. Hurlbut, a man they had known only as the dead husband of the widow from whom they'd bought the house two years before. Robert remembered how she had wept with a certain sentimental pleasure as she showed them the garden, sad at the thought of leaving the house where she and her husband had lived for years, but unable any longer to deal with the grass and weeds and cleaning. Her husband had been dead for four years, she had told them, and she had struggled to keep up the house, but now she must leave.

The letter had been opened, and Robert picked it up and read it.

Simpson Ward
St. Mary's Hospital
Dear Road
Scarborough, Yorks.
23/10/70

Dear Mr. Hurlbut,
    I regret to inform you that Miss Jane Hurlbut is very ill.

As we have no particulars regarding friends or nearer relatives than yourself perhaps you could let us know your wishes should anything happen in the future. She is well cared for and although she does not have visitors she is not short of anything. I shall be pleased to hear from you.

Yours sincerely,
H. Thompson (Ward Sister).

Robert folded the letter and put it down. Was it the man's sister? Not likely. A cousin perhaps, the reference to no nearer relations suggested that. Whoever she was, the man was dead and his widow had disappeared. Mail was returned from the forwarding address she had left.

The letter would never be answered; the old woman would die, not short of anything and never having visitors. She had never married. Her life had meant whatever it had meant, and now she would die alone. His own father lay dying closer by.

The front door opened. Robert turned and saw Jennifer in the hall taking off her coat. Her face was wet from the rain, but as she turned and saw him, it became tense, as if waiting for anger.

"We came back early," Robert said. "Cindy got sick."

"What's wrong with her?" Panic, only just held back.

"I imagine it's 'flu. She threw up at the hotel. I wrapped her in a blanket and put her to bed when we got home. She seems to be having chills so I made a hot-water bottle."

"Did you phone the doctor?"

"Not yet. She said she didn't feel that sick. You talk to her and see what you think."

"Where's Gavin?"

"Downstairs. He didn't get much of an outing."

The return of the family worries had changed Jennifer's face, dried from it some small flood of light, and as Robert looked at her, she seemed older than he'd ever noticed before, more tired. No wonder the house was a mess.

"I noticed the letter from the hospital in England," he said. "I couldn't think what to do with it so I opened it. Then I wished I hadn't."

There was a silence. Robert thought of the old woman dying in that English hospital. He and Jennifer had shared what now seemed a lifetime. They were close to the country of the old, refugees standing at the border stations never knowing if what they had salvaged from the past would be what was needed for this new country. Yet he must enter the country, Jennifer must, taking with them only what they were, whether it was of any use at all.

Help me, Jennifer, for the sake of all the pain we gave each other.

Jennifer looked at him, and he couldn't meet her look.

"I'd better go up and see Cindy," she said.

He nodded and turned to leave. He must go to Elizabeth. He and Jennifer were imprisoned in a past that left them mute. With Elizabeth, with her rare intensity, something large or terrible or grand was possible; he must find that, he mustn't give up now and enter humbly the kingdom of the old.

He got in the car, which seemed to travel without his volition to the house where he would find her. He entered the familiar hall and went up the stairs. He could hear her voice; she was talking on the phone. He stood in front of the door, uneasy at the thought of meeting the presence at the other end of the line. They would know each other. He could feel the other presence already.

He knocked. Elizabeth's voice stopped. Her soft movement crossed the room. The door opened and they faced each other; she wore her long dressing-gown.

"I'll just be a minute," she whispered. Robert stepped into the room and closed the door behind him. Again, as always, it was like entering a new kingdom where time and space had different proportions from in the world outside. A blue pillow lay on the white bedspread and seemed to make some statement about all this. Elizabeth was sitting in the white wicker rocking-chair with the black phone at her ear.

"It was just somebody returning a book," she said. "No I'm fine, really. I've been reading a lot of French stuff."

She denied him so easily. He could feel her mother on the other end of the line. The room was tense with the knowledge of her. He pictured her sitting in another house, a crease at the side of her neck.

Elizabeth's feet stuck out in front of her. They were long and thin and pale. He could feel the texture of the skin. He turned back to the door and depressed the light switch so that the room was dark except for the bit of light that came through the closed curtains. Elizabeth's voice moved in the dark, cheerful and matter-of-fact.

Robert walked to the bed and stood beside it, taking off his clothes, feeling that Elizabeth could hear what he was doing, feeling her voice in its mimicry of friendly conversation touching his skin. When he was naked, he pulled down the covers and climbed into the bed. He lay still and listened to her voice. It excited him. He lay absolutely still, blood beating in his chest.

"No, not next weekend, Mother. I can't. Yes, I know he drives up all the time, but I've made other arrangements. Of course I want to see you. How's Philip? Is he still training? Is that his best time? Great. Okay. I'll see you soon. Don't worry. Bye."

Robert heard the phone set down.

"Robert, what's the matter? You look shaky."

When he didn't answer, she crossed to the bed. Her hands moved over the bed until she found him, then one began to massage the back of his neck.

"Get in."

"What's the matter?"

She sat for a moment, then stood up. He could hear her take off the dressing-gown, the brassière and underpants she wore underneath. She slid under the covers, and Robert turned to her, drawing her to him, holding her by the neck and waist, kissing her silently. He would not let her deny him. She drew her mouth away.

"Robert, what's wrong?"

He forced her mouth back against his, began to turn his body to hold hers down.

"Robert? Please."

She sounded frightened, but he could feel the fear exciting her. He took her skull in both his hands and held it tight and still. She tried to move away, but he held her.

"Robert?"

Her breath was fast and as he entered her she was soft and wet, but her voice was fearful.

"What is it? Talk to me."

He went on in silence, concentrated, willing her fear, as if his movement in her could set fire to the intensity of that feeling, fear on the edge of something else. To break through, to break through, to break through. Then he came, still hard and fierce, and he lay lapsed, and she began to cry.

13

Coming out of the movie, he touched her, and she drew away.

"What did you think of the show?" he said.

"I'm not really sure."

"Too many brooding closeups."

"I suppose."

Then silence. The street, the house, the door, the stairs, the room, the silence. Her tall, almost awkward body standing by the window looking out. Robert went and put his arms around her. It was like embracing a tree.

"What's wrong?"

"I don't know."

"You must know."

"I don't."

"Was it something in the movie?"

"No."

"What then?" His hands moved trying to provoke some reaction. There was none. He took her shoulders in his hands and turned her around to look in his eyes. They were bright, empty. He tried to kiss her, but she turned her face away.

"What is it, for God's sake?"

"You want to kiss me, and I don't want you to. Does that mean there's something wrong with me?"

"You usually want me to kiss you."

"I don't now."

"Are you going to send me a letter when you do?"

She shrugged. Robert felt himself disoriented. He didn't know where he was or what was happening; in his head there was a singing, he was outside his body and his words seemed to play themselves out in front of him like a script. He looked at her face and felt a terrible intense consciousness of each feature. Her nostrils, the scar beside her eye. It all bent itself toward a powerful pressure of desire and he took her in his arms and moved her toward the bed.

She struggled, without speaking, and there was a strange interlude of breathing and effort. He didn't know if he wanted to penetrate her or to kill her.

She got free of his arms and stood staring.

"What's going on here?" he said. "What kind of craziness are we involved in?"

"You want to hurt me."

"I want to give you pleasure."

"That's what I mean. It sounds like an operation. You operate on me and give me pleasure. It's got nothing to do with me."

"Of course it has."

"Just because you say it has."

"I feel that it has."

"I don't. I want to run away from you. You're dangerous to me. The other night when you were so angry."

"You wanted me."

"That wasn't me. I wasn't there at all. Didn't you know that?"

"No."

"It's true."

"I don't know what you mean. I don't know what you're saying." Robert could feel a tightness in his throat as if an animal was trapped there.

"You want to say that things aren't there because you can't see them," she said. "If you say it didn't happen, it'll go away. What I'm afraid of isn't there if you say it isn't. You're like my mother telling me that a nightmare didn't really happen. It did happen. It happened to me. This is happening to me but you say it isn't. It is. It is."

Her face was distorted from holding back tears. He tried to touch her but she pulled away; he could feel the anger in all his muscles. He wanted to hit her. She was right; he did want to hurt her, but she had made it happen.

There was a small plate on the dressing table beside him. On it were a few crumbs. His eyes focused there and were still. His fingers moved over the edge of the plate. Something overflowed its boundaries, and he lifted the plate and smashed it on the floor. She turned to the noise. They both stood there in silence, unmoving, like stone.

"Please," she said, "leave me alone. Please. I really need to be alone."

He turned away. He was nowhere.

"I'll phone you when I get back from Toronto."

She said nothing. He had been dismissed again. Like a schoolboy. He felt unable to breathe or swallow as he went out of the room and down the stairs. As he reached the outside door, it opened toward him, and a fat girl came in. She jumped at the sight of him, then smiled. Robert ignored her, let himself out and pulled the door behind him.

It was a cold night, and he shivered. There was nothing to do but walk home again to his empty apartment, so he did that, carefully not looking back up at her window. She would draw the drapes and be closed into the silence of herself, where no-one would interfere. That was perhaps what she wanted him for, someone to flee, something to make her silence important, necessary. Driving him out left a space, and she could play in that space.

He wanted company but was afraid of any company he might find. Ray Statler would patronize him, Jennifer would be awkward. He thought of Wilson and remembered that Edith was out of town. He turned at the next corner and made his way toward Wilson's house; he couldn't stay long, but he couldn't go home alone tonight.

There was little light in Wilson's house, but Robert knocked anyway. The study was at the back of the house and Wilson was likely to be there reading or working. Robert knocked and stood shivering.

He saw a light come on. Wilson came to the door.

"Robert, how very good to see you, do come in."

"I remembered that Edith was away and thought you might not mind some company."

"Always glad to see you, Robert. Any time at all."

Robert was filled with absurd warmth by the old-fashioned courtesy of Wilson's manner. He knew that he would have said the same to anyone, but it did make him feel welcome. He needed such gentleness.

"Could I make you a drink, Robert?"

"Please, Wilson."

"Gin, isn't it?"

"Gin is perfect."

Wilson made the drink and they went into the study. It was

a room that Wilson had added at the back of the Victorian brick house in place of some kind of shed or summer kitchen, and it was on a lower level than the rest of the house. Robert walked down into it, into a kind of comfortable detachment. He sat down with his drink and thought how good it was to be here with the older man. Why was he possessed to beat his body against the raw flesh of that bright-eyed child? He could sit here forever.

"You look overwrought, Robert."

"I may be. I'm going to Toronto tomorrow to see my father, and I'm not looking forward to it."

"Living alone is very trying. I'm lost without Edith here. Find I'm at a loose end constantly. Does it trouble you, living alone?"

"Sometimes I'm lonely. Now and then I like it."

"You're still a young man. Many things are still possible for you."

Robert just nodded. That ought to be true, but he was discovering how few things seemed possible. To say that character is fate is fine as an aphorism, but to discover it, to live it out in the fact of entrapment in your own personality with its recurrent failures is another matter. He would have liked to believe that he could perform some act of moral levitation, raise himself by his bootstraps to become a new, a better person. Being Robert Mallen was not the best fate that he could imagine. But it was his fate.

"Is anything happening about your book on our recent crisis?"

"I've given it up. My friend in Parliament was quite hostile to my ideas and, without him or someone else in that position, it wouldn't be interesting. That's one of the terrible things about it. We're all just passive observers. The eyewitness reports of a lot of passive observers aren't all that interesting. We all know that we're worried and helpless." Robert was detached from what he was saying. It was true, but he didn't care. The fight with Elizabeth had shut him off from his own feelings.

"I suppose it's possible to get eyewitness material from Montreal."

"But the really important thing is what happened in Ottawa," Robert said. "What do *they* think is happening? For most of us it's happening in a foreign language. It's like watching a movie without subtitles. And Trudeau says, Oh, I speak the language, I can interpret for you. And if necessary he'll fire the projectionist. Because we don't want to watch movies that we can't understand. We want what's safe, what's familiar, our own room with everything in place." Robert couldn't tell what had led his mind back to Elizabeth, whether some logic or only the pressure of his anger.

"Kidnapping, murder," Wilson said, "they're terrible things, especially for an idea. It's not fashionable to believe that ideas are dangerous, but some ideas are like a disease. Like a body that starts to devour itself. All this anger, all this distrust."

There was such comfort in Wilson's voice.

"But what he's doing is like using surgery for a case of small-pox. The operation was a success but the patient died."

"Perhaps, Robert. Just how strong is the fabric of our civility? We don't know. If the whole thing were in a book, you and I would know how to deal with it, we could show how it was wrong, but as it is, it's very puzzling. Would you like another drink?" Robert was frightened by this, by the truth of Wilson's insight.

"One more and then I'll go."

Waiting for the drink, Robert sat with his eyes closed, his mind swollen with desire for Elizabeth's body. He had allowed his desire to be reawakened, and now it wouldn't let him alone. Pale skin, dark hair. Light in darkness and darkness in light; she was shining and frozen, cold and bright. *Quelques arpents de neiges*: a cold country.

Wilson came back into the room and handed him another

drink. He began to talk about Ray Statler. It was very clear that the young man upset Wilson and made him uneasy, but his phrases were carefully chosen to avoid any apparent hostility. Robert grunted and nodded and sipped his drink. He imagined his hands on Elizabeth's body. Did Ray Statler have problems with his Slovak princess? Not likely. He wouldn't stand for them. He'd simply throw her out and reach for another goddess. To have that absurd confidence. Wilson's voice had stopped.

"He's difficult to work with," Robert said, "but it's probably worth it. He has talent."

"No doubt of that. No doubt at all. I suppose I just find him a bit hard to understand. He sometimes gives the impression of having been raised in a particularly seamy beverage room."

"I know what you mean."

"I shall make the effort to understand him, but of course as soon as I have any success I'll find that he's leaving the press and going somewhere else. It all makes me feel my years, Robert, and I resent that."

"We just begin to get used to the fact of being who we are and suddenly discover that it's harder than we thought."

Wilson sipped his drink and smiled.

"Very nicely put, Robert. That's very much how I feel about these recent bouts of illness I've been having."

He nodded and looked off at a bookshelf as if savouring the taste of the drink or the thought. Robert looked at the curious pale face of the man; Wilson was not in good health, and when you looked closely at his face it showed, but somehow his manner, his discipline, kept you from noticing the sense of strain. Robert wished that he himself had such dignity.

"I think I'll make my way home, Wilson."

"No need to hurry off."

"It's late, and I'm off to Toronto in the morning. I really must go."

"It was good of you to come by."

Robert picked up his sweater, and the two men walked toward the door. Outside it would be dark, cold. He didn't want to leave but did, and made his way home.

When he reached the apartment, he couldn't settle down. He walked impatiently from room to room, picked up the phone, dialed the first five digits of Elizabeth's number, then put it down again. He paced, stared out the window.

I have reached the end of another beginning. I must choose now, to go on somehow, to make a new world, or to give up. I need the faith to have faith.

He slept fitfully that night, partly because he knew the alarm would wake him early for the train. The night provided no real break between one day and the next, only a bridge of confused dream images, and the morning brought no renewal, only a sequence of mechanical gestures, to rise, dress, drink coffee, drive himself to the train. Sealed behind glass, he watched the landscape unwind, mile after mile, bleak or dark or rich under the veil of November damp. He tried to read, but his stomach curdled and he returned to staring out the window.

Somewhere in the journey, the thoughts of Elizabeth began to fade a little and thoughts of his father, of Marion moved into his brain, as if the air itself held their presence, growing stronger as he got near Toronto. The last time he had seen his father, he was in the hospital just after the stroke. There had been nothing to say. For months before, his mind had been playing strange tricks in what might have been a comparatively early senility or a suddenly manifest psychosis. Conversation with him was jagged, confusing, dependent on whether you thought he understood your words. Robert had talked. His father had talked. That was all.

When Robert had left home at 21, it was with a great sense of relief and release. His father had always thought him a failure, and Robert was content to let that evaluation stand, since it helped him to be ignored, invisible. It was better than anger.

The train moved past the small brick houses of Toronto's east end. It was a part of the city that was strange to Robert. He had lived in Toronto for many years without knowing the east end, and now he watched with a strange fascination as the train passed by house after house, life after life. A woman pushed a child in a stroller. Two men walked through a yard full of scrap metal.

When they reached Union Station, Robert resisted the temptation to go to a restaurant and get something to eat. There was no use postponing the visit. He got a cab and gave the driver the address. They turned north up University, that strangely wide, unreal street, passed the monumental heaviness of the legislature. Was someone in there talking about James Cross or Pierre Laporte? He wondered if there were soldiers on duty.

Within a few minutes they were stopping in front of the large brick house where Robert had spent his childhood. Not an unattractive house, he thought, unless you knew the people who lived in it. It was odd to stand at the door knocking. This had been his home.

When the door opened, Marion stood there, a heavy woman in a blue sweater and dark blue slacks, holding a Siamese cat in the crook of her left arm and staring at him.

"Hello, Robert," she said.

She reacted almost as if he wasn't there or was a stranger. She held the door for him, not looking at his face. As the door closed behind him, something else closed on him, a whole lifetime of feelings. The umbrella-stand beside the door, the watercolour with its blue Mediterranean sea and blue Mediterranean sky, small figures suggested by a few brushstrokes, the mirror that hung at the end of the hall; all these things, familiar from his childhood, seemed to focus some emotion hidden in Marion's impassive welcome, holding him in some knot of feeling that had been tied a lifetime long.

You have left me alone to come into this house of barren

pain. My mind is all tangles and confusions because you have rejected me now when I need you. Elizabeth, Elizabeth, virgin queen.

In the mirror at the end of the hall, Robert could see the two figures, his own and Marion's, caught in an awkward photograph in dark tones, two figures seen in a moment when their only relationship was avoidance of each other. The focus of the picture was the face of the cat, narrow, beautiful, tensed with readiness to jump, the eyes somehow too large, too aware.

"Come into the front room," Marion said.

She turned and went in through the doorway, and something in the movement of her body as she crossed the room made her human and hurt. There was a stiffness in her shoulders. He remembered that she suffered from arthritis, and he could respond to her physical pain, that it hurt her to move.

"How are you, Marion?"

"Don't ask stupid polite questions, Robert. Do you want a drink? I do. I know it's too early. I drink. I suppose you know that, although you've been out of touch enough that maybe you don't. What will you have?"

"Gin and tonic."

"I don't have gin. It's a cleaning-woman's drink."

"Whatever you've got."

"Scotch."

She put the cat down on the chesterfield and got a bottle and glasses out of a small cupboard that sat against the far wall, beneath a print of the Lake District that his mother had brought back from England many years before. What had that cupboard held when he lived in this house? Back issues of some magazine. The *National Geographic*.

"Do you want ice or water?"

"Both."

She walked out of the room past him, her shoulders still held with that odd stiffness, but her heavy legs giving a sense of power to her movement. In the emptiness of the room after she left, Robert's eyes moved hesitantly over the furniture, the round table in front of the window, the leather armchair, the sofa where the cat lay curled on the brown upholstery. In the corner, another Victorian chair covered with maroon cloth. He remembered the figure of Marion curled in that chair, a young girl reading, her hair long and dark.

His sister walked back into the room, gave him the drink. Her hair was short and grey. She picked up the cat and sat on the sofa, holding him in her right arm, her left hand stroking him, heavily, as if she wanted to feel his bones move. They sat and drank in silence until there was a sound of movement upstairs. Marion looked up toward it.

"His nurse," Marion said. Their eyes met.

"I think he's asleep," she said.

"Is he lucid?"

"Now and then. Not very often. You'd have to come around a lot more often than you do to catch him in one of his lucid moments."

The stiffness in her shoulders seemed to cause her to hold her head at an odd angle.

"Isaac was asking after you," she said.

"You've seen him?"

"He calls from the office now and then. He feels it's his duty. I don't know why."

"How is he?"

"He seems happy. I think he chose better the second time."

At one time Robert and his brother-in-law had been close, but that was fifteen years before. In another country.

"He married another Gentile," Marion said. "It's getting to be a habit with him."

She took the cat in both hands and threw it roughly to the floor.

"You're 40," she said, "and I'm 43, and here we sit in this familiar room waiting for our father to die. Where we sat 25 years ago listening to him scream because I was about to marry

153

a Jew. You didn't say a word to defend me."

"I was afraid of him."

"So was I. But I thought if I rebelled and married Isaac I'd be free. Didn't work, somehow."

She opened the cupboard and poured more Scotch into her glass.

"*You* have kids," she said.

"That I don't live with."

"Don't feel sorry for yourself."

"You do."

"I'm an alcoholic. It's part of the game."

"Are you?"

"I don't know. I drink too much and for the wrong reasons. Probably I am. When he dies I'm going to go to Italy. Isaac took me there for a holiday once, and I liked it."

"Is he going to die soon?"

"God, I hope so. There's nothing for him to lose, and it won't be any loss to me. I'm not here because I like him."

"I want another drink," Robert said. "I'll go out in the kitchen and get my own ice and water." He wanted to get out of the room. Marion's truthfulness was too much for him. It always had been. Robert had never fought openly with his father, had always tried to maintain some kind of facade of affection. He preferred politeness, dishonesty. Tell them what they want to hear. While he admired Marion's harsh courage, it made him uneasy; some wounds didn't need to have salt rubbed in them.

In the hall mirror he approached himself, a dark long figure, features unclear in this light. Turned to the left and pushed open the swing door that led to the old-fashioned kitchen. He couldn't walk into the room without expecting to see his mother. Standing by the counter. He found himself superimposing the body of his mother, remembered, on the body of Marion, as in one of the proofs of congruent triangles. They fitted. Their features were altogether different yet something in the overall shape was the same. Robert didn't know why he should be surprised, but he was.

The smell of the kitchen was the same. A curious smell. Warm? Cool? The kitchen smell. What the child smelled coming home from school and walking into the empty room. It only had this smell when it was empty, when there was no smell of food.

He put ice and water in his glass. He didn't want to leave the kitchen, for there was some curious comfort here, his mother's presence asking him what he had done at school today. In the front room Marion would be in her favourite chair, reading.

He went back into the front room.

"How's Jenny?" Marion said as he sat down again with his drink. She was watching the cat, who washed itself gracefully on the other end of the sofa.

"She seems all right. She has a job teaching part-time in one of the high schools. I don't really know how she is. She doesn't tell me, but then she never did tell me much. I to request, she to deny."

"It was your own fault."

"You would say so."

"You never saw her as a real person at all."

"I've heard that line a hundred times, and I'm still at a loss to know what it means. Could we talk about something else?"

"Do you have a mistress?"

"Something else."

"Nice weather for November."

Grey cloud and you, the queen of snow. *Quelques arpents de neige*, your white unattainable body. Snow. A few acres of snow.

"Do you have nurses all the time?"

"Not at night. He usually sleeps, and if he doesn't I can go in and listen to him rave."

"What does he rave about?"

"Everything. He sounds like Hitler."

Robert stared down into his drink as if truth could be found there.

"Poor Jenny," Marion said. "You must have driven her mad. You're such a subtle coward. You make me admire Isaac. Poor simple man, he was."

"I imagine he still is."

"Yes, he is. And he phones me once a week to make sure I'm all right. He's like some good Jew out of Dickens."

Robert could feel the alcohol lifting him so that he didn't care about Marion's anger. He could accept it. Now was the time to see his father.

"I want to go up and see him now," he said. He took another sip of his drink and then set it down. He'd need it afterward. Marion drained her glass as she stood up. Robert stood waiting for her to go out the door.

"Go ahead," she said. "You know where he is as well as I do."

Robert went out the door and turned toward the stairs. Up the stairs. He must have gone up these stairs to bed a thousand times as a child, but he couldn't remember any particular time. At the top he turned the wrong way, what had before been the wrong way, toward his parents' two bedrooms, not his own. He entered his father's room, and the nurse stood up, a small efficient motherly woman who seemed to have resolved any unnecessary bumps on her personality into the uniform and the role that went with it. It was her job not to be seen as a person, only as a function.

Robert did not look at his father, concentrated on the nurse until Marion walked into the room. She introduced Robert and asked the woman if she wanted to go downstairs for tea. He was left alone with the body in the bed, forced himself to look.

It looked almost gentle, asleep or unconscious, that face. It had always been the face of a stranger, so the age and pallor and transparency made it no more strange. The hair was still thick. It didn't seem that the man could be senile, on the point of death from a failing heart, and have such thick, iron-grey hair. The senility had come on quickly, or so it seemed, although as Marion always reminded him Robert hadn't been around long enough to know. There had been failures of memory, small irrational acts earlier. At times Robert wondered if it wasn't senility at all but only a late blooming of a madness that had been kept hidden in his father's rages and solitude. He had always been a difficult, solitary man. Sometimes it seemed as if his ordinary social being was a thin mask over something more terrible.

Robert looked down at the big hands that lay outside the covers. As a child he had been terrified of those hands; when his father summoned him for some sort of inquisition, the hands were all he could look at, the stiff hairs on the back drawing his eyes until his father would shout that he must not avoid his glance. He would look in his father's eyes, which were grey and opaque, like machines for seeing.

As he stood by the side of the bed Robert was thankful that the eyes were closed, that he did not have to meet them. The nurse had turned on a bedside lamp. Robert turned it off and stood, more at ease, in the grey light of the room. His father's room. Always from his earliest memories, when his father was away, he would go into his mother's room with her. He would hold a skein of wool on his two hands as she drew the wool and rolled it into a ball. In the evening she would knit with the ball on the floor beside her; she would knit Robert a sweater. He couldn't remember his mother's face, except at the end of her life when it was raddled by the merciless pain of the cancer that killed her. He could assemble a face, feature by feature, as if in a puzzle, but it was not a living face that he remembered. Did she really have her tea-leaves and her palm read almost weekly? At the time it had seemed natural, and now unbelievable. Most children suspect at some time that they were adopted, or have some moment of suspicion that their parents are not real; Robert had somehow managed to take them for granted, keeping himself hidden, being himself unreal, so that he could avoid that fear. Now, at 40, he saw them as puppets, strings of atoms wholly foreign to his consciousness. It was not just unbelievable that they had made love and produced him, but that they had been conscious, been there at all. He had seen their clothes, their gestures. Nothing else.

He felt a chill of fear, of loneliness. Elizabeth's face, gone miles from him, refusing him, calling him a stranger. He wanted comfort, he wanted someone to hold him. He could feel his childhood in this house, and it was a lie. His mother was a closet full of dresses.

He reached his hand out and touched the hand of the man in the bed. The eyes opened and looked at him, fierce, unknowing, unforgiving. Robert spoke, but there was no reaction to his words. The lips in the strange face moved, but didn't speak. The eyes held him. The lips began to move again. Sound moved toward expression, toward words, found its shape.

"Go away."

The lips closed. The eyes closed. Robert began to feel dizzy and took hold of the bedside table to steady himself, closing his own eyes and breathing deeply until the vertigo passed. He turned away from the bed and walked down the stairs, into the the front room where he swallowed the remains of his drink and poured more Scotch into the glass.

He could hear the voices of Marion and the nurse from the kitchen, and he didn't want to meet them, so he stood by the front window and sipped the Scotch straight. In a few minutes the nurse would go back upstairs, Marion would come in and find him. She had her father's fierce eyes; he didn't want to meet them.

Robert took a large swallow of whisky that burnt his throat, then he put down the glass and walked quietly to the front door. Let himself out, walking slowly down the front walk, and then when he reached the sidewalk beginning to run until he came to the corner. He stopped there and looked around him, unclear as to what he was going to do. For a moment the streets were empty, grey, frozen. He shivered and pulled his shoulders up. A woman walked out of a brick house across the road and turned toward him. He turned down the street and began to walk, quickly so that his thoughts kept moving, couldn't settle into the memory of the house, the memory of Elizabeth.

Just keep walking. The only cure for fear and trembling is movement. Run, walk, screw; only if you are brave enough, think, sit still and look and think, like you old man, setting out from Vienna, writing the Gestapo an ironic letter of recommendation.

Robert found himself on Avenue Road and turned downtown, without any clear intention, only aiming toward something familiar. This was always the direction he had gone, to work, to the university, to plays or concerts. Down the hill to Bloor, toward the beacon of the Park Plaza. Where he had proposed to Jennifer. Where he had taken several other women. He walked down the hill toward Davenport. Remembered a girl named Eileen whose last name wouldn't come back to him. She had come to work as some kind of editorial assistant, a tall, striking, big-breasted girl. They had sat in the bar on the roof of the Park Plaza one night and she had told him the usual kind of thing that girls that age told you, family, school, ignorant young men. There was a moment of silence and she had turned to Robert and said, "You're not using me, you know, I'm using you." Within a month she quit her job and disappeared.

As he walked, Robert realized where he was going, not the Park Plaza, there was no point in drinking more, but the museum. He loved to go there, always had from his childhood on, and the sense of the past, the lovely impersonality of all that ancient wreckage calmed him, took him out of himself.

He walked more quickly now that he knew his destination, and the museum occupied his mind. When his father's face appeared, looking up at him, he could put it aside. His parents were strangers to him. What had seemed so new about that thought? That his father was a harsh, distant man who had never much liked him was not something he hadn't known. There was no way of knowing that the old man knew who it was he was seeing.

My dying father sent me away. I am a free man. I am not necessary to any single being on earth. I am a free man.

Near Yorkville a couple of tired-looking kids asked him for money but he brushed past them. He didn't want to speak, didn't want any human contact. He walked fast, ran up the museum steps, paid his admission and stood in the rotunda, breathless, almost afraid now that it wouldn't work. Straight ahead of him now a gallery of armour, on the floor beneath Indian artifacts, glass cases where plaster figures built fires or scraped skins, stiff bright-eyed figures that had haunted his boyhood dreams.

Robert turned to the staircase and went up one floor, then into the gallery that housed the Greek antiquities. He stared at the warm pink colours of the clay in the figures, the rough texture of the surface. He stopped to stare at an archaic face of a woman, a goddess. Impersonal, expressionless, distant. A clay face that was some absolute conception of divinity. He remembered the girl who said she was using him, remembered her body, the flat nipples on her big breasts, her body glowing in some kind of dim light. She had no face, she was as impersonal as this ancient goddess. He had never been to Greece but once a friend had told him of the terrible barren beauty of the Greek sunlight. The face of the goddess was as simple as rock. A desert of rock and clay. Marion said he had never seen Jenny as a real person. No. Of course not. Nor ever could. She was a landscape. What he was to her he couldn't know, but she was a landscape with its own gods and goddesses. It was not personal, never had been or could be.

He walked on, walked on. The figures burned into life in his eyes. Through the Greeks back in time, falling backward to Egypt, the figures on the mummy cases purer, clearer. Language and geometry met in the simplicity of the hieroglyphics. Robert's stomach burned and his mind ached for these things. He stopped at a glass case and saw Bastet, the cat-headed goddess, the goddess of war. The world was speaking to him in all these images today. He saw them all as goddesses, Marion, Jennifer, Elizabeth, every woman he had ever known spinning round him in a hieratic stillness. Walked on past the marble statue of a Roman matron, solid, pragmatic, eternal.

Robert went back to the stairs and up to the top to another of his childhood favourites, the gallery of stuffed animals and birds, bright-eyed, absurd. He confronted the huge stuffed moose and introduced himself. All the rich variety of the animal world in glass cases. Hello moose, hello mole, and newt and badger.

In front of him was the figure of a young girl, perhaps only thirteen or fourteen but with the first suggestion of maturity in the way she held her head, moving the long hair. Without really intending to, Robert began to follow her, fascinated. She glanced in the glass cases without appearing to pay much attention until she reached the hall at the end of the gallery, where there was a set of small tanks with live fish. She walked around it slowly and stopped when she came to the tank holding two piranha. Robert moved slowly toward her as she stood there, and he was only a few feet away when he saw her move her face toward the glass. Her pink tongue moved out and pressed against the glass just in front of one of the fish, and the fish, half the size of a child's hand, opened its fierce mouth and lunged against the glass, trying to get at the pink flesh. Robert could see every detail of its multiple teeth as the girl moved her soft tongue in and out teasing the fish to come back and back against the glass.

It was unbearable. Robert turned and walked away. The girl was the same age as his daughter. He could not bear the brilliant sunlight of what he saw. It was too hard, too impersonal, too absolute. He wanted no divinities. As he walked down the stairs he thought of Cindy, and decided that he would go to the store in the museum basement and buy presents to take back to her and Gavin. There were lots of oddities for sale there that they couldn't get in Kingston.

But the museum hadn't quite finished with him. Behind the counter of the small shop was a girl of eighteen or twenty who immediately brought Elizabeth into his mind, as an image evoked by this girl, not a real person but a presence, a particular fate. The girl was smaller than Elizabeth, not really like her in detail, eyes brown rather than green, but it was something in the cleanliness, the poise. Everything about her was neat, expensive. Perfect white teeth, the only makeup a little eye-shadow. Her manner was quiet, pleasant. Her father would be a doctor, a lawyer. There were many others like her, but that was part of the shock of seeing her here.

Pale skin, a neat small body. A few acres of snow. That whiteness was a fate as terrible, as unforgiving as the face of that archaic goddess. It was that. Unforgiving; it was that in women that he had felt today. Beneath the level of friendship or warmth and compatibility, they were perfect and absolute and wholly unforgiving. Unknowable, like the lost memory of his mother, faceless.

He bought a book on reptiles for Gavin and a polished rock necklace for Cindy. The girl smiled at him. He didn't smile back, just paid his money and left, standing on Avenue Road until he was able to hail a cab to take him to the railway station. He drank in the Royal York until train time, fell asleep on the train and was wakened by a terrible dream in which Elizabeth was dead.

14

I will get over this, she told herself. Sit still here in the dark. Remember Grandpa's farm, the room in the old house before they moved, the open place on the hill behind the cottage.

The farm: the smell of the cattle and the milk. On the farm it is always summer because she only goes there to visit in the summer. The room where she sleeps is small, and there are always one or two flies buzzing over the ceiling. She picks daisies.

The phone rang, but Elizabeth did not answer. She didn't want to talk to anyone. Whenever she saw Robert, they fought. He had come back from Toronto changed. Or she was changed. There was nothing to be said now; no longer did she find any rest in his eyes. When he came near her she grew stiff and distant.

All she wanted was to sit in her chair and be at peace. It was dark and windy outside and a streetlight illuminated the bare branches that waved in the wind. She had been sitting in the dark for a long time. Her hands were folded in her lap. Her mother had taught her to sit that way in church. In Kingston Elizabeth did not go to church; she didn't know why and regretted it.

On the wall of the room is a picture of a girl. She has a silly face, and there is a lamb beside her. Elizabeth wonders if it is little Bo Peep. This used to be her aunt's room. Aunt Sally. Elizabeth puts the daisies she picks in a jar and puts them on the bureau.

Robert was out there somewhere in the city. It was Robert who phoned. Or Burtch. She didn't want to talk to them, to any man. Who would demand and demand. Her bones were like ice now, and she was untouchable, so little present in her body that she felt as if she might be made of glass. Men were lost and hurt, brilliant with pain, and they blamed her. Said they must find comfort in her. Didn't see that she was glass and ice.

In the corner of her room in the old house, the house where she was little, is a closet. Elizabeth can walk into it and close the door and then she is nowhere. Her father smiles at her, but he is keeping a secret. He looks at her and thinks she knows. Her mother is angry at something, but Elizabeth does not know what. No-one is supposed to notice. Elizabeth can sit in the closet and think about other people. She talks to them and there are no secrets.

Burtch when he had hit her: his face swollen with rage, his hand sudden. The scene unfolded in her mind, each moment turning for her to watch it. All his affection changed to hate, or revealed as hate. It was not Elizabeth he saw, but something else that fitted his need. A gentle shadow that warmed him. He hated her because she was not that gentle shadow. When his hand struck her, the most surprising thing was that she felt no pain. He slapped the body that stood in her place, and she watched, observing the mask of hatred on his face.

The hill is steep and the climbing difficult, over chunks of granite and through thick bush, clumps of cedar and juniper tight and close to the ground, but they go up each day and reach the top where there is a clearing, a patch of pink granite covered only with moss and lichen. From here it is possible to see three lakes, Bent Lake directly below them, and Wild Duck Lake and Roger's Lake to the west. She and Martha pack sandwiches each day and climb here. They bring books and pieces of paper for writing poems or letters. It is quiet. Sometimes they talk and sometimes are silent; once Martha talks about her mother's drinking, but Elizabeth hates to hear it and wills it to be forgotten. One day while they are there storm clouds blow up and there is a heavy rain. They take off their clothes and dance naked in the rain, whooping like Indians. Elizabeth feels that the gods of the earth and sky are close, are touching her skin. They laugh and hug each other, their skin slippery and wet, and they run into the shelter of the woods to dress.

The street was cold and windy and empty. There was a feeling of snow in the air, and Elizabeth was glad she had worn a heavy sweater under her jacket. Even with that she had to run to keep warm, running past the church and the courthouse and down toward the water. As she passed houses, she glanced toward the lighted windows; inside life went on, usual, rich, predictable. Outside, she ran through darkness toward the lake. She had a curious feeling that she could turn to one of the houses, walk in the door and simply begin to live. She would know what was expected of her. Her husband would be understanding. It would all be simple and proper.

She passed a big brick house that reminded her of her grandfather Ross' house. Her grandfather Ross was an Elder of the church. Elizabeth remembered when she was young she had wanted to know how old you had to be to become an Elder. She thought it must mean that her grandfather was the oldest man in the congregation, so she was not surprised that he died when she was still a little girl.

Her mother's life was right, her mother knew best for her. Her mother smiled and was kind and pleasant, and in that way she made the world better, less frightening. Her mother understood her best. Her room at home was always orderly and kind, with pictures in it of all the people she loved. In those pictures Elizabeth was happy.

Now Robert hated her. She could feel his hands on her skull as if he wanted to crush it. He wished to destroy her; his gentleness was a mask to draw her close to him. What did her face look like when her body grew bright with desire? Once she had opened her eyes and glimpsed Robert's face. It had looked swollen and concentrated. It looked like Burtch's when he had hit her. The person was gone. It was primitive and terrible, uncaring.

It was not what she wanted. She was not like that.

She stood at the edge of the lake and shivered as the cold

wind cut through her clothing. As the waves splashed against the cement wall drops hit her face, and she enjoyed the sudden consciousness of her skin. Would Robert understand that? He would listen and nod, then reach for her to make her feel desire, to make her dance for him. He was so insistent. He went into her as if she were anyone. He took no account of her.

A man was walking along the sidewalk toward her. She stared out at the water, willing him not to speak to her, but she knew he would. It was almost as if he were a messenger. As if she were waiting for him, but she didn't want to know whatever he had to say. She wanted to run, but if she ran he would follow her.

He was an old man, shorter than Elizabeth by three or four inches. He stood beside her and looked out at the lake.

"A cold wind," he said.

"Yes," she said. She stared out at the lake imagining that she was out there, deep under the water, cold and safe, free.

"What's a pretty young girl like you doing out here on such a cold night? I suppose you're like me, want to get out and get a breath now and then. I do a lot of walking at night. Don't sleep too well anymore."

Elizabeth didn't speak. His voice was pleasant, but had the automatic quality of a man who lived alone and was used to talking to himself.

"Are you a student?" he said.

"No," she said. "I used to be."

"I took you for a student. Working, are you?"

"No."

He waited for her to explain. She was having trouble finding words. Each word had to be forced out, lifted like a weight to her lips and then expelled.

"Do you have a boyfriend?"

"No." She felt it to be true.

"Should have, pretty-looking girl like you."

"No."

"I live alone myself, since my wife passed on. I'm pretty good at batching it, you know. But it gets lonely. You must get lonely sometimes too. I'll bet you do. I'll bet you really do get lonely."

"No. I like being alone. I'm happiest when I'm alone.".

"A girl your age. Sounds to me as if you've had a bad experience." He pulled his coat tighter around him. "That's a cold wind. Wouldn't surprise me to see snow. I'm pretty good about the weather. Comes of growing up on a farm. My wife used to swear by me, said I was better than the radio at telling the weather. It's just a feeling. I don't know right where it comes from, but it's there."

"It must be interesting," Elizabeth said. It was her best attempt at conversation.

"It's awful cold standing here, isn't it? My apartment's warm though, very comfortable. Aren't you cold? You must be, you're not dressed very warm." He coughed. "I better be getting on home. Would you like to come home with me? Pretty girl like you shouldn't be going home alone." He patted her on the arm. Elizabeth didn't answer him, she couldn't.

"I'll make you a cup of coffee. I've got some cookies."

"No."

He patted her arm again.

"Why not? There's no harm in it. Some company for a lonely old man. I could tell you a few things. I've learned a few things. I'm a sort of student. Of human nature." He was standing close to her.

Elizabeth drew away.

"I have to go now," she said.

"I'll give you $20," the old man said and took hold of her arm. "$20. That's a lot of money. You could use that."

Elizabeth tried to draw her arm away, but he held tightly.

"$25," he said. His face was close to her now and he was pulling at her arm. He was too close, and her free arm rose and hit him hard twice in the face. There was blood where her nails hit him. He dropped her arm and his face changed. He was crying.

"You knew what you were about," he said. "Standing out here in the middle of the night just waiting for someone to come along. I know your kind. Too damn good for the rest of the world. Butter wouldn't melt in your mouth, I suppose. Damn young whores."

Elizabeth turned and began to run, his voice following her, she panting and running fiercely to escape. It was too much, unbearable. She thought she could hear his feet behind her and didn't stop to look back until she had run two blocks. She turned and looked. There was no-one there.

I will get over this, she told herself again. It will change, and I will laugh at it. I will get over this.

She did not believe it.

15

The fourth day. She was gone, vanished; now he could think of nothing but that she was dead. He saw her hanging from the closet doorway in her room or lying cold in the bed. He tried to remember her words the last times he had seen her, tried to remember some detail that might give him a clue.

For the first day or so, he had thought nothing of it. He assumed that she was out, perhaps avoiding him. The second night, he had begun to worry and had trouble sleeping. The next day he had tried her home number in Ottawa. Her mother had said she wasn't there and gave the operator the Kingston number, obviously puzzled. The third night, unable to sleep at all, he had phoned her apartment and then gone there in the middle of the night. He had stood outside her door at three in the morning, knocking loudly and thinking of the story of how she had set out to drown herself. The moonlight on the clouds.

Elizabeth dead in the moonlight. He had gone back home and, sitting in his room staring at the shadows cast on his wall by a streetlight, he had thought of Wayne Burtch, thought that of course she must be with him, jealousy and relief moving through him at the same time. He knew it was too late to phone and went to his bed, but as soon as he lay down he began to worry. He saw her dead. He saw the young man's heavy body mounting her. He saw her pale body moving along in the cold water of the St. Lawrence.

Robert got back up and got Burtch's number from information. As his fingers moved around the dial he tried to prepare something to say; the absurdity of what he was doing struck him and he hung up. He sat with his face in his hands trying to make sense of what he felt. Whatever she had done, she had done because of him. And. Whatever she had done, she didn't want him to know. And. She had planned this for him. His fingers dug angrily into his skin. It was all madness.

He picked up the phone and began to dial again. Forced himself to dial all the numbers and wait as it rang and rang.

A voice, foggy with sleep. Robert stumbled over words, embarrassed. Burtch hadn't seen her. He hadn't seen her for days. He hadn't heard from her. He knew nothing. Robert felt better, worse. She was not in Burtch's bed. All the more likely she was dead. He apologized. Burtch said to let him know if he heard anything; he was obviously concerned now, felt like a friend and Robert was ready to babble everything in his mind, but stopped himself out of some kind of pride.

He looked in a drawer and found some old sleeping-pills. Took two and lay rigid in the bed, watching the ceiling as if she might appear there, projected out of his eyes onto the dark screen by the intensity of his consciousness of her. He woke into daylight, unrested, dopey from the pills. He got out of bed and walked through a series of gestures that he thought he knew. These were the things he did every day, dressing, shaving, but he didn't recognize them, didn't seem to know the face he met in the mirror. All day he sat at his desk trying not to think. Would his call to Ottawa make her mother curious? Would she too start to look for her, phone, get no answer? If Elizabeth wasn't found, there might be an investigation. Police. Her diary. They might accuse him. What if her body was found in the river? What was said about him in her diary? It drove him mad. No-one would believe him (for who would? Who knew him well enough to believe him? Jennifer, who never believed him). He gave more and more complete, more and more absurd explanations.

The day went on. He hardly tried to work, although now and then he would make the gesture of picking up a pencil and making marks on paper. Outside the window it was dark and cloudy. It looked like snow, high tumbled black clouds moving fast. He stared at them, beginning to get drowsy. Let his eyes close.

Drifting images. A voice talking seriously about something. Investment freezing. He drew near the crowd with the feeling that he would be less noticed there. A face turned toward him and looked back away through the crowd at whatever was the focus of attention. He knew what they were all looking at. Someone asked him a question he didn't understand. The crowd was moving, fading away somehow and he was alone staring at a lump of mud. The lump of mud began to wiggle and a face appeared. It was the face of a baby that stared up at him. He knew it was dead, but the terrible knowledgeable eyes held his. It was Molly's baby. He tried to reach it and couldn't.

Robert opened his eyes, awake and frightened. Ray Statler was standing in the doorway of his office.

"You look awful," he said.

"I dozed off."

"What's the matter?"

Robert just shook his head.

"Look. I'm taking off for the rest of the day. You look as if you could stand a drink. If you feel like it, come round. Margita's away so I'll just be sitting round playing with myself."

"Thanks, Ray. Maybe I'll come round later on." He sat still as Ray walked down the hall and out of the building, then went to the door of his office and closed it. Completely alone in the silent room, he felt more in control.

He went and sat in the chair behind the desk and stared out the window. If only he could talk to someone, but there was no-one he would talk to. Elizabeth? Yes, perfect if he only could. Jennifer? He couldn't go to her now, like the child she had always thought him. He wondered about getting Molly's phone number and calling long distance. Foolish.

Robert looked out the window, concentrating on the movement of the clouds as if they were telling a story. Would the snow come? A picture came into his mind. Brueghel, the illustration of the blind leading the blind. The one face was like the face in his momentary dream. Outside the room, there were thousands of faces like that waiting to look at him. Their mouths moved. His mouth moving on Elizabeth's. The panic of drowning, lungs full of water and consciousness spinning away into a last thread of light.

He held himself in his chair and willed time to pass. The smallness, the total inconsequence of his being, the few quirks and habits that made up his personality, the simple chemistry of his existence; it seemed like nothing. In a way it helped, to feel so unimportant. What happened to him could not matter.

He got up and went to the closet in the corner of the room. He put on his heavy cardigan and the old raincoat he had worn over it. The way he dressed was absurd, comic in its carelessness. The raincoat was wrinkled and stained. That made him feel good. He felt warm with it on. No-one else would wear it like that. He felt as if he existed.

Outside there was a cold wind, but Robert turned down toward the lake. He had to go and look at the water and think of her there, if she was there.

The water was dark grey and the waves were running east under the power of the wind. The water looked dangerous and the island was a long dark line, without clear detail. Robert slid through the iron pipes of the fence and jumped down onto the rock at the edge of the water. A wave splashed him. He bent and put his hand into the water, and looked at the white flesh, swollen in the lens of fluid. He thought of her now, for a moment, purely, as if he himself did not exist, thinking of her so intensely that it was as if he could feel her pain. It was as if he had never seen her before, and he sobbed. Took his hand out of the water and wiped the cold water on his face. The wind, striking it, chilled him. He climbed up to the sidewalk and made his way back to his apartment.

When he got there, he mixed a drink and phoned her number. It was a ritual now, he expected nothing but the automatic sequence, ring, silence, ring, silence. He hung up, then sat with the drink, his chair turned so that he could look out the window at the grey street and the brick wall on the other side. He saw a girl go by, clutching her scarf to her throat against the cold wind. It was the time of day when people went home from work; they always did this, every day at this time. There was a pattern to things, light and dark, work and rest. A time to plant, and a time to pluck up that which is planted. Nothing ever changed. Laporte was dead, Cross was free, Charbonneau and the others were in Cuba. Trudeau had got away with it. Elizabeth was gone, like a ghost that had blown across in front of his eyes and vanished. They would ask him about her death. He could see the detective, a man his own age, with a son and a daughter. How would he answer? It wasn't like that at all. But was it? For her. He didn't know. He knew how he felt when she looked at him, what his response was, but hers? He knew nothing. His eyes were closing.

The telephone rang. He woke, confused. It was dark now. The phone rang again. He picked it up, as if only to stop the noise.

"Listen, come over here and have a drink with me instead of sitting there brooding."

"Ray?"

"Of course."

"Maybe later, Ray." He wondered what time it was. It felt late.

"Oh for Christ's sake. I don't know what's going on, but you've got the look of a man with woman problems. The only solution is booze."

The voice hurt him with its confidence. He wanted to draw away.

"It's good of you to worry about me, Ray."

"Yes it is. I'm a wonderful warm-hearted person. Are you coming over?"

Robert didn't want to. He wanted to be alone. Still that seemed to be doing him no good.

"All right. Maybe I'll come over for a little while."

"Good." He hung up abruptly. Robert sat listening to the dial-tone as if it were music, then suddenly put it down. He got up, and prepared to leave the apartment in a series of hurried gestures. He moved, these days, in sudden bursts, feeling that otherwise he would subside into an endless lethargy. They would say that Elizabeth was his victim, but she had damaged him too. He had met her while saying to himself that he wanted no more pain and guilt, and she had drawn him on to destroy her.

The snow had begun and was falling steadily. He shivered when he reached the street, and the shivering did not let up until he'd reached Ray's apartment. Robert had only been there once before, and he nearly missed the door. Ray had the whole top floor of an old stone house, and the rooms were higher than attic rooms usually were. Robert was thankful that the building seemed warm, and the shivering stopped. He knocked at the apartment door and Ray shouted to him to come in. He went in and up the stairs.

There were two drawing-boards in the large front room and there was that curious mixture of order and disorder that artist's studios often had. On the walls there were batiks, pieces of old wood-carving, and a patchwork quilt in various colours of red. One section of the wall was covered with drawings of nudes. Robert recognized Margita's long dark hair and dramatic face.

There was a record playing. Ray motioned Robert to a chair and reached for a bottle.

"I've only got Scotch," he said.

"Scotch will do."

Robert looked again at the drawings on the walls. Their precision surprised him, seemed unlike Ray. If Margita had not been a beautiful girl, the drawings would have been cruel, for they had a kind of hard detachment that made the girl look even more an exotic princess. Some of the poses were almost at the edge of obscenity, yet they remained under control, held by some alchemy in the personality of the girl or the talent of the man. They were brilliant.

"Isn't she a nice piece of cunt?" Ray said, handing him a drink. Robert turned toward him.

"Don't look surprised. Like Renoir said, you draw women with your prick."

"Is that how you drew those?"

"Sure. You're surprised they're good, aren't you? You figured me for just a loudmouth."

Robert wondered if Ray was drunk. There was an edge to his voice.

"Where is Margita?" he said.

"Off visiting mummy and daddy. Just look at the fur on her. Like a bloody animal. You could get lost in all that hair."

Robert drank from the glass. The voice rubbed against his nerves like sandpaper. Ray sat down in a chair opposite him, his legs spread, his hand stroking his beard as if enjoying the texture. For a few minutes they sat in silence. Ray reached down beside him and turned up the record.

"What is that?" Robert said. He knew only a few of the contemporary groups.

"Perth County Conspiracy."

"What names."

"I've always wanted to hear of a group called Syphilitic Blindness."

Robert did his best to smile. He felt strangely comfortable here. The place was so attractive. And after a while you didn't have to listen to Ray any more.

"That girl I met at the party giving you trouble?"

"Not exactly."

"She will." He got up and went to the bar beside him and mixed another drink. "I could tell to look at her. Jesus, I hate that kind of women, professional virgins. I could tell to look at her. All that unnatural glitter in her eyes. And she wants you to feel that. If she did open her legs it would be like fucking green apples." He took up his glass and drank half of it. "Can I draw you? You have a nice face when you look so worried."

"No," Robert said. "Not now. I want to be invisible."

"Drink up then." He came and got Robert's glass and filled it again even though it wasn't completely empty. Robert watched him pouring the whisky and wondered about the intensity of his attack on Elizabeth. What had set him off? Robert's eyes moved to the drawings. As Ray brought him the drink, he saw where Robert was looking.

"Do you like them?" he said.

"Yes. A lot."

"Think I'm a coward to be a designer instead of a real artist?"

"Never given it any thought."

"I have."

He sat back down in his chair and stared at the drawings. He lifted his elegant patterned tie and began to chew on it. Robert was surprised by the gesture. It didn't seem to belong.

"I only have one subject," Ray said. "Female flesh. And I don't think that's enough to make an artist. Nude, number 42,000."

For a few minutes Robert had been able to forget Elizabeth, but now, the thought of her came back as a real physical chill, a positive sensation of discomfort. He was afraid. For himself. What was in her apartment?

Ray turned over the record. Words went past, but Robert didn't hear them or take them in. He sat and drank and thought about the strangers reading her diary. He was hurt for her too. She was so private.

"Do you want to talk about it?" he heard Ray saying.

"No." Ray gave him another drink. He was starting to feel drunk, a little privately hysterical.

"Get the fuck rid of her," Ray said. "That's what I'd do." He turned the record up louder, then talked louder to be heard over it.

"I think Wilson's going to die soon," Ray was shouting. "I've seen that look before. My old man looked like that before he died. I think it's the look you get when you know. Can't describe it, but you can sense it there."

The voice seemed to go on and on. Robert stopped listening and drank what was given to him. All his attention was on the thought of Elizabeth's apartment. He must know what was in it, if she was there, dead. There must be some way to get in. He would go in and find her, and then phone the police anonymously. After he had taken away her diaries if they mentioned him. They must mention him.

A plan began to take shape in his mind. He would break in, through the door or window. He must. He must know.

Robert stood up, and realized that he was a little drunk. Everything was at a distance except his need to get into the apartment. He made his way to Ray's bathroom, emptied his bladder and splashed cold water on his face. He felt better now that he'd made a decision. He felt almost calm.

When he came out there was a girl standing by the door, and Ray was taking her coat. She was a pretty girl with a slightly round face and light reddish hair.

"Robert, this is Anne."

Robert nodded toward the girl and said hello. They all stood still.

"I must go," Robert said.

"No hurry."

"No. I must go."

He picked up his coat and made his way to the door and out. He tripped on the stairs and nearly fell, but his hand reached out in time and stopped him.

When he reached the street he found it was still snowing. He walked back to his apartment to pick up a screwdriver and put on running-shoes, then made his way to the house where the stairway led upward to her room.

Ahead of him, through the falling snow, Robert could see the house, a light on in the downstairs hall showing the thin columns of the old wooden porch. He had a picture of the porch breaking and falling on top of him, of himself crawling away through the snow with a broken leg, crawling as far as the park and freezing to death there under the statue of the World War I soldier, staring up at the black figure against the black sky.

Where are you, Elizabeth, why have you done this to me? This is madness.

Robert stopped on the corner opposite the house where Elizabeth was not, where perhaps her dead body lay, or some clue as to where she was. The lights in the bottom apartment were out. That was good, for he couldn't imagine climbing those porch pillars, knowing that within two or three feet there were people awake and listening.

He looked at the house. The snow moved in the air like the flickering consciousness of his fear. But he couldn't go on, not knowing, waiting for someone else, for her mother to come, to search her apartment, read her diaries. What had she written? Would he look and find some stranger who was hidden in words he misheard, in the long pale body against which he'd pounded his own in a futile attempt to drive her out of the boundaries of her own head?

Anger surprised him. He wanted to cross the road and smash the windows of her room, break everything in it. He felt a little dizzy.

A car came toward him, and the snow glittered in its headlights.

You see, Elizabeth, I was frightened of what might happen if you were dead, if you'd killed yourself and I was somehow responsible. No doubt I should have the courage to hold my head up and say, well, she was a grownup and took her chances in the world, but I'm not courageous now, if I ever was, and I'd rather sneak out of it, slip out the back door with my trousers half on, not to be caught.

You see, old father Freud, I'm not your equal, never will be.

Robert crossed the road and walked up to the door of the house, a familiar walk up the three steps, pushing the door without needing to turn the handle, walking inside, to his left the leaded glass of the coloured window with the picture of the effeminate knight, turning and walking up the stairs, and finding himself at the door of Elizabeth's apartment. He tried the door. Knocked softly, afraid that someone might answer.

He looked at the door and lock and wondered about the possibility of forcing it. But there seemed to be no way to do it without making it obvious that the apartment had been entered. He heard a door open on the third-floor landing and someone come out and start downstairs. Quickly he turned away and ran down the stairs, moving softly enough that he was sure he wouldn't be heard. When he reached the bottom of the stairs he turned into the dark hallway that led to the door of the ground-floor apartment and stood silently against the door, while a blond girl in a dufflecoat went down the stairs and out the door. His heart was jumping as if it planned to leave his body, and he stood there for a few minutes trying to calm down. To distract himself he decided to recite limericks, but the only one he could remember was the young lady from Niger and he wouldn't recite that because he'd always thought it cheated on whether the "g" was hard or soft. He began to giggle at the absurdity of his situation. He was terrified.

When he was sure that the blond girl would be out of sight down the street, he came out of his corner and moved toward the door. Without any light from outside, the stained-glass window was just a dull silver with vague traces of pattern in it. He stood and looked around the hall, and everything seemed to have become dull and far away. It was all unreal, and he didn't care about it, about anything, but he went on automatically. Out the door.

That house was always overheated, so that as soon as he found himself on the porch he began to shiver. Felt in his back pocket for the screwdriver. Now he must do it.

He climbed onto the low railing, wound his legs around the post and began to shinny up. Within a few seconds, breathing heavily, he was at the top of the post, but he found himself against the porch ceiling and, unable to see how he was going to get onto the roof, he reached out and felt a piece of eaves-trough that was loose in his hand. It wouldn't stand any weight at all. He tried to stretch his arm to lift himself. For a few seconds he hung there, then he slid back down the post and stood on the porch. Again his lungs and heart felt too big for his chest. There was a car coming up the street toward him. He walked down off the porch and away from the house, down to the corner, where he crossed the street to come back toward the house. As he walked slowly back, shivering continuously now, his running shoes soaked from the snow, he studied the porch, to see if there was a way to get to the roof. As he reached the corner opposite the house, he noticed, by the light of a street-lamp hazed in snow that the eavestrough was missing from the

179

far side of the porch. He'd instinctively made for the dark side away from the light, but on the side nearer the street, he'd be able to reach upward from the post and get a solid grip.

You see what you've driven me to, Elizabeth. Like a knight of romance I climb to your window. Shivering and wet and afraid.

Robert crossed the street again. His shoes were like a swamp. But colder.

The street was empty as he crossed, and when he reached the porch again, he climbed on the rail and, with a kind of desperate energy, shinnied up the post and reached out over the edge of the roof. His hand stretched behind him and upward, and it didn't seem that he'd ever have the strength to lift himself up and out over the edge of the roof and back in onto the roof again. He hung there, in a furious desperation, his legs aching from clinging to the post. It would need an acrobat to get up to the roof.

Determined, convinced he was going to fall, he put both his hands over his head and back to the edge of the roof. He used them to slowly raise his body, while still clinging to the post with his legs. He hung with his back to the ground, ready to shatter his spine when he slipped. Snow was falling on his face, and his teeth were chattering. He edged his way upward on the post and stretched his arms out across the roof until his fingers found something solid; it was a wooden rail that surrounded the roof. Robert's fingers crept forward until he had both hands on the rail. He pulled it toward him to see if it was solid. It seemed to be.

Robert was panting and shivering and felt as if he was about to cry. Holding tight to the rail, he loosened the grip of his thighs on the post and let his trunk slide downward, but still he held to the post with his feet while he pulled on the rail and gradually scraped his body around the edge of the roof, getting purchase with his elbows, shifting his point of balance, lifting and pulling upward until he was on the edge of the roof. He climbed over the rail and stood panting. He could hear voices down the street coming toward him. The snow was still falling, and the lawns were covered.

He walked to the other side of the roof, taking out his screwdriver. He tried to see into the room, to see if she was there, dead, hanging or drugged. He could see nothing without going in, and there was a storm window. He hadn't thought of that. Fortunately it was only held in place by four turning catches on the frame. Robert moved the catches and using his screwdriver loosened the window and lifted it out of the frame. He put it against the wall, and then realized that he couldn't leave it there. It would be seen, and he'd have the police here. He'd have to take the storm window in with him.

He turned back to the window and put his screwdriver under the edge of the sash and pried it up. It opened easily, he lifted it wide open. There was a curtain in front of it, and he pushed it aside, then lifted the storm window and turned it sideways to go through the frame. He set the window down on the floor and climbed into the room.

It was dim and hot. Empty. There was no pale body stiff in the bed or hanging from the doorframe. Robert turned and closed the window behind him. He was still shaking. He drew the curtains closed and crossed the room in the dark to find the light switch.

He opened the drawers of her dressing table, and his fingers, terribly conscious of every movement, explored them, searching for her diary. He found nothing. He looked on her bookshelves, in her clothes closet. Everything seemed to be in order. The closet was full of clothes. She was here and not here.

Robert turned to the closed door of the small bathroom, went to it and pulled it open. Empty again. Not sure what to do next, not even altogether sure now why he was here, Robert sat down on the toilet and stared ahead of him. For a long time, he sat there, not thinking, just letting the heat soak into him. Around him there was a faint smell that he recognized as the smell of Elizabeth's skin. It must be bathpowder. Robert sat and took in the smell, finding her there by not finding her; by not finding the corpse, pale and stiff and bridal, he almost found her living presence.

Beside him was the shower cubicle. Where she had stood naked in the gamut of hot water.

He stood up and began to take off his clothes. His body was almost warm now, except for his feet, and as he took off his shoes, he wiggled his toes with the odd sensation that he might feel them drop off. He turned the shower faucet against the far wall, turned on the hot water, then the cold, adjusting the two, then stepping into the cubicle he turned the faucet down on himself and stood covered by water. It poured down over him. He felt that he was dressed in Elizabeth's body, her shadow held him, and he drew in breath deeply through his nose and smelt her skin.

He stood in her tall pale flesh. She melted like snow. He saw her floating in the icy water of the harbour, a long white fish moving in the currents, whirled into a dance like life by the engines of the Wolfe Island ferry above as it pulled out into the night and chugged its repeated way to the island. The lights of the ferry moved away on the black lake. He stood at the edge, his sword raised as his lady turned in her snow-whiteness.

The water turned suddenly cold, and Robert reached for the knob, skinning his knuckles and grunting with pain before he succeeded in shutting it off. He stumbled out of the cubicle and found a towel. He rubbed himself briskly.

Dry, he walked into her room. It was pale, still, like a shrine. Her image. By the window a desk, painted white, drawers down one side. On it a photograph of Elizabeth and her father taken several years before. The wicker chair, white, with a dark blue pillow. On a dressing table, Noxema, cold cream. Kleenex.Along the edges of the mirror letters and invitations. A rosette of bright-coloured ribbon. In the mirror he saw the torso of a naked man, cut off at thighs and shoulders. Thin;

body hair dark brown.

Robert stared at himself reflected in the mirror as if he didn't recognize this male intruder, naked, hairy, hung with genitals, out of place in the stillness. His mind reflected the room and hated his body's intrusion into it. He turned away.

He had left the closet door open, and as he turned, he saw the rack of clothes, saw the clothes hanging on their rack like limp abandoned personages. Robert walked to the closet and put his hand into the privacy of the clothes, feeling Elizabeth's presence against his skin. He could smell her. His hand moved over the slightly rough texture of the long green paisley dressing-gown. He remembered his hands taking it off her, and as he did, he reached into the closet and peeled it off the hanger. It hung across his hands and he lifted it to face him. He put his arm in the sleeve and drew it on. The other. He felt her presence in him. His penis began to heat and fill with blood. He stood with his eyes closed, the robe held tightly around him. He was nowhere. It was like being on stage in a huge amphitheatre before an audience of silent smiling gods.

There was a knock at the door. Robert stopped breathing. Did not move, tried to stop the noise of his heart and blood. The knock was repeated. He listened. He thought he heard feet going away down the stairs, then decided he had imagined it. He stood still, counting seconds until he came to 300. He moved quietly toward the door and lay on the floor beside it, his ear against the wood. He could hear nothing.

For some reason, he imagined Elizabeth standing out there in the hall, not the police, or her mother or a worried friend. He could see her. She was wet for she had come out of the water, and she was shivering with cold. Robert felt dizzy and faint and out of his head. Breathed slowly and deeply. He could hear the water dripping from her hair. There was something trapped in the back of his head, making his ears sing. His stomach began to twist with nausea, and he scrambled across the floor, no longer caring about the noise, reaching the toilet and vomiting until his stomach was empty. He lay on the bathroom floor, cold and sweating, rocking slowly back and forth.

Slowly, heat and strength began to come back to his body. He climbed up, flushed the toilet and walked into the other room. He took off the dressing-gown and put it away, and sat down on the bed to rest and gather his strength. He felt simple, convalescent, like a child encountering illness and recovery as mysteries. He put on his clothes, as if he had been told to. Put on his coat and wet shoes. Gloves.

He went to the door and let himself out, without much thought of who might be waiting. No-one was. But when he was in the hall, he became frightened again and rushed down the stairs and outside. He started to run down the street, then stopped himself and walked slowly. Look normal. People don't run down the street at this hour of the morning. He walked aimlessly for a while, then stopped to look at his watch. It was after 3. He walked, not toward his apartment but toward the lake, then when he realized that the lake was ahead of him, turned another way, through the university campus. It was still snowing a little, and his feet were beginning to chill. He saw two black figures, their arms around each other, move through the glittering snowflakes under a streetlight. He walked on past the hospital, hurrying, for hospitals were bad luck.

His feet moved on through the snow like two strangers who were leading him somewhere. He watched them. Foot, foot. Step, step. This went on for a while until watching them began to make him dizzy. He stopped and stood still. His feet stood still. He opened his mouth as if to speak to them, admonish them gently.

Instead a howl came out of his chest and lifted his head until it pointed to the sky and accepted the cold bright baptism of the snowflakes. The sound seemed to go on for a long time. When it stopped he stood still, looking up at the clouds that were low and swift and reflected the city's light. He looked around him, but the street was empty. The lovers had vanished.

He turned and walked. Purposefully now. The house drew him, Jennifer's house, where his children slept like good animals. When he reached it, he stood for several minutes on the street outside, looking at the dark windows. There was nowhere else he could go, and he must go somewhere. He was a man who belonged in a house; the streets were not his home.

Robert went up the path to the door and knocked. If one of the children woke and came to the door, what would he say? He knocked again. There was no response. He knocked again, harder. A light came on upstairs. He waited. Knocked quietly. Jennifer appeared, her face heavy with sleep, drawing an old purple dressing-gown around her. She opened the door and he walked in.

"What is it, Robert? You look dreadful."

He nodded, but found that he didn't want to talk. He tried to smile at her, but the enterprise was not a great success. He looked down at her heavy dark comfortable body. The puffy face. Perhaps this was where he belonged.

He reached out to her and drew her toward him. She came, but not naturally, not easily.

"Are you alone?" he said.

"The children are here." There was something a little hostile in her voice.

"She's disappeared," Robert said. "That girl. I think she's dead."

"Why do you think that?" Her face turned up to him.

"I can't find her anywhere. It's been four days. She used to talk about suicide sometimes. There's nothing to do."

"You're shivering."

"I've been walking a long time. My feet are soaked."

"Take off your shoes. I'll make you some warm milk." She drew away from him. Robert sat down in the chair beside the door and took off his shoes and socks. He remembered that Jennifer thought he had ugly feet. He took off his coat and sat in the chair, staring at her.

"Come in the kitchen." He followed her obediently. He didn't want to fight; they could fight later. Right now he was comfortable just to be somewhere. Later he could decide whether it was a good idea.

Wise men, fathers, have patience with me. Tomorrow I will examine my principles.

Robert sat down at the kitchen table and watched Jennifer move around the kitchen. There was something a little large about all her movements that had always excited him. It was probably the first thing he'd noticed about her, that and her large breasts. Now that her body had filled out they were less obviously striking, but when she was young, she had been one of those women who had to learn to live with a constant shifting of men's eyes to her upper body. In high school it had been a source of embarrassment to her.

She poured the milk into a cup, stirred in sugar and brought it to the table. She sat down across the table from him.

"That girl didn't strike me as the sort who'd kill herself."

"Well, she's gone."

"Don't her friends know where she is?"

He shook his head.

"I did all the obvious things, Jenny. I even broke into her apartment to see if she was lying there dead. She's just vanished. She may be in the lake."

Jennifer reached out her hand and put it on his.

"Poor Robert."

He wanted her sympathy and resented it. She found it so easy to be objective, to sit back and smile and be friendly. Why couldn't she be hurt to lose him? Everything was so easy for her.

She left her hand resting on his, and he turned his hand over so that they were holding hands across the table as he sipped the hot sweet milk. It felt good in his mouth, and the warmth began to move through his body. He drank it greedily.

"I feel a little better."

"Good."

They sat there in the familiar kitchen in the middle of a winter night holding hands.

Robert felt the pulse moving in her wrist.

"Can I stay here?" Robert said.

She shook her head.

"Why?"

"I don't want to confuse things any more."

"You want everything simple."

"No hope of that."

"You never really wanted me."

"Let's not argue, Robert."

She stood up from the table. He thought she was going to walk away, but she came toward him. She held his head against her body.

"Come to bed if you want," she said. "I'll hold you and warm you and make love if you like. But I don't want you to be here in the morning. I don't want to start trying to please you again."

Robert put his arms around her, greedy for her warmth. She felt so sure and solid.

"Make me warm," he said.

They walked up the stairs, entered the bedroom, took off their clothing with a curious slow formality. They made love as ghosts might, at ease in their bodies because they were no longer tied to them.

Afterward, Robert was warm. They lay quiet and Jennifer stroked his face.

"I feel good, being here with you," Robert said.

"But you have to go home now," she said. "Phone me if you hear anything about the girl."

Robert got up from the bed. He was already far away. He put on his clothes in the dark, walked to the bed and put his hand on Jennifer's hair, then went out and down the stairs. He wondered if his children could sense his presence there through the armour of their sleep and dreams.

He put on his wet socks and shoes and went out. The snow had stopped now, and the ground was pure and smooth. There were no car tracks, no footprints except his own. He walked up the street toward his apartment. He felt invisible, as if he had spent the night being someone else or as an eye, watching. He was the snow, the long empty street, the trees drawn in fine white lines on rich black paper. His feet rose and fell. The snow made everything silent. He could hear the sound of his gloves brushing against the edge of his coat. The house beside him had a light on in the kitchen window, and he could see a dark shape moving inside. It must be morning. He looked east, and the sky was beginning to become light.

When he reached his apartment, he felt so tired that he thought he couldn't walk up the stairs. He opened the outside door and leaned against the wall until he had the energy to search his pockets for his keys, but the energy didn't come. He willed each action individually, to take off his right glove, to put the hand in the pocket of his coat, to move it until it struck the metal of the keys, to take it back out holding the keys, to move to the door.

Up. Another step. Up. Another.

He reached the top of the stairs and took off his coat and shoes, then walked to the front room of the flat and stood at the window. The sky was almost blue now, and in it he saw the thin white crescent of the new moon.

The new moon, phase of the moon as virgin, showing only the pale edge of herself. The lost lady. What he had seen of Elizabeth was the pale edge of the crescent moon. Not the circle of its fullness, not the globe of its being, its circle in space.

He sat down at the table in front of the window. She was in him now, wherever else she was, dead or alive. He took a pen and paper and began to write her a letter. After he had done that, he would sleep.

Three

Dear Robert,

What words are there to write to you, from here, so far away? I feel as if you are someone I cared about long ago. A thousand years passed during that flight over the Atlantic. I am here with Martha, and that is where I should be, now anyway. I am lying on the floor in front of the gas fire, and Martha's feet are on my back. Martha says there is little fog in London anymore, but there is some today and I'm glad.

I ran away. That's what you would call it, and perhaps you're right. I don't know. I remember I was sitting in my room in the middle of the night trying to think about you and me, about what you wanted from me, and why I was so afraid. I opened a drawer and started to look through some old letters from Martha that she sent me two months ago, saying to come anytime. I couldn't think right when I thought about you. I didn't know who I was or why. There seemed no point going on and on. It was too dangerous. So I packed a bag right then at three in the morning, and as soon as the bank opened, I went and took out all the rest of my money and got on a train to Montreal. I ran away. Now I'm here, and you are a thousand miles, a thousand years away.

I am at peace here. Martha holds me in her arms and I am at peace. Oh, I know how angry that will make you, all the things that will come into your mind to say to me. You will accuse me, maybe you will be right, but that is not given me to know. I know what is right for my head and my bones, that is to be here, now.

In my memory you are scarlet and quick, a flash at the edge of my eye. You take my quiet room and turn it askew, turn it on some strange angle, fitted to a different universe than mine.

If I had not gone, I would have wanted you to kill me. I seemed to owe you my blood. I know I am young and I don't understand anything.

Will you write to me if I send you my address? Martha says I shouldn't do that, but I might. I'd like to hear from you. A voice from the past, a voice from another country. I think of you fondly. Don't be too angry with me, I'll feel it even this far away. If you care about me, you must want my happiness, at least a little, and I am happy here.

Yesterday we went sightseeing. Today we're going to the British Museum. It's all rich and safe and marvellous. I suppose I'll have to go back some day, maybe soon, that I'll have to settle and live my life, get married, do all those things. I don't know.

Will I do that? Will I see you again? And what will you say? Those things seem so far away. I wish I could explain to you what I feel here, that Martha knows me, does not require too much, does not put me in danger. I suppose I prefer danger only in my poets. There isn't enough of me to stand it if it comes close.

The gas fire flickers. It is translucent and makes me remember how I felt to be near you. At first I thought you would help me with that, but you wouldn't, didn't. So I have sought my peace here. I didn't run home to my mother and the memory of my father, isn't that a little brave, can't you like me a little for that?

I couldn't bear to be like that, blue and flickering, a transparent flame. You wanted to destroy me.

Someday I will find my way. Perhaps I already have.

I think of you often and affectionately. You are vivid. Too much so.

All my best,
Elizabeth.